Share Taxi

and Other Semi-True Tales

Jerry Harwood

Sale Creek Publishing

ISBN: 978-1-7347874-6-7

Contents

Share Taxi

1 Faustin jerked awake in his chair and instinctively swatted at his arm. In the dim light from his single desk lamp, he saw a cockroach hit the ground. It bounced on impact and then landed on its back. The creature's legs were desperately writhing as it sought traction. Faustin looked around and realized he and the cockroach were alone in the third-floor office. Behind on his notary work, he had stayed after hours. What used to be a rubber stamp if someone had paid their fees was now a political nightmare. He was required to sift out any Tutsi papers that might have made it into the queue before April 7th. He couldn't recall when he fell asleep but apparently, it was on one Ntakirumana family. He stacked his papers neatly and placed them in the wired "incoming" box carefully. The precarious mound was higher than the mesh sides of the basket and threatened to topple at any moment. As he rose from the desk, Faustin wiped his eyes getting the sleep, that is what his mother always called it, out of the corners. Removing the palm of his hands, Faustin blinked a time or two trying to convince himself to wake up for the trip home. It was then he again looked at the cockroach.

Faustin raised his foot over the bug and paused. The office mores was to kill them on sight. Some co-workers even made sport of the tiny carcasses. The place was infested. However, this particular one had the distinction of waking him up. Realizing he might have woken to the jeers of his office mates in the morning Faustin's worn sole now towering over the impotent bug held its position. Then, as if given an officially sanctioned reprieve, his boot averted to the side where he gave it a gentle nudge. The bug slid across the floor but remained upside down. He again nudged it with his boot. This time the bug tumbled, found purchase, and was gone.

"Ungrateful pest," Faustin uttered with a smile threatening to overtake him.

2

Taking his coat and briefcase, he walked down the stairs and into the streets of Kigali. It was dark, perhaps close to midnight. Twegeranes, roughly translated as "share taxis," would not be plentiful this time of night. Faustin knew hopping the two he normally used would take several hours or more since they often waited till their passenger seats were nearly full before departing their station. Instead, he got in the queue for one that ran slightly north of his home. It did not require exchanging taxis, and he could walk downhill through the woods the half-mile or so after drop off. There was a well-marked trail where some of his neighbors trod the path daily.

A few minutes later a Toyota minibus with "Muzic Pleze" written on the side and music notes decorating the otherwise brown exterior pulled off the road into the loading lane. Stepping into the share taxi Faustin paid his fare and found a seat on the third row. Right before they departed a woman and her young daughter scurried on to the bus from a nearby building's alley. She hunched low as she ran and Faustin thought if she stood straight, she would likely be a head taller than himself. Likely she had Tutsi blood on her mother's side. Her father must be a registered Hutu for her to be out in public. Although the lateness of the evening suggested, her story might be complex. As she and her daughter stepped into the share taxi Faustin committed in his mind not to ask. She headed for the third row and placed her daughter on top of Faustin's briefcase, positioned like a ready-made high chair on his lap. She gave him a short smile that asked if this was acceptable. Faustin smiled back agreeing to the non-verbal contract without speaking. The woman edged her bottom on to what little seat remained in the row. She placed a finger over her lips, instructing her daughter to remain silent. The girl obliged.

A man in the row ahead turned to look the woman up and down with longing eyes that perhaps hovered their insatiable gaze a bit too long in certain places. "It is late for such a pretty lady to be out. Not safe. Lots of soldiers and others out that would take advantage of you these days."

He smiled a smile that was half kindness and half threat. The woman looked down, not making eye contact. She did not respond, and the man turned back to the front of the share taxi. The silence set the tone for the ride.

The share taxi drove a mile or so and then pulled off to pick up additional passengers. Per customs of courtesy, passengers exiting did so expediently before new passengers entered. Then the share taxi returned to the road. Then another stop, and then a third. On the third stop, one person exited, and a couple entered. As they were finding seats, the woman seized her daughter and stepped fervently out of the Toyota. Faustin watched as the two again hunched over made their way into the shadows. All watched, but none spoke. Talk entangled. These were dangerous days as Hutu soldiers continued the war against Tutsi rebels.

Faustin had taken this trail to his apartment before and had even done so at night. But the killings had changed the landscape. Several heavy trucks had been through and had torn asunder the bushes and trees he previously used as familiar guideposts. The trail itself seemed unclear and trodden over. He worried he was becoming lost, maybe even to the point of not being able to retrace his path. Relying on the fact that the entire journey was downhill, he continued what most resembled a true path forward. Faustin was buried in his own thoughts, trying to remember his path when he was startled. Awaken again to his surroundings, he became motionless.

"Help!" There was a sobbing that punctuated the cry. "Help! Sir! Help!"

Faustin dropped his briefcase and extended his hand to a nearby tree as his legs began to buckle. There was no light and no visible silhouettes. The voice was muffled, and the tears moreso than the words pierced the night's canopy of silence.

"Stay silent. Please. Talk entangles," Faustin thought.

"Help!" came the tearful voice.

Before he made a decision in his mind, Faustin's body moved right, toward the sound. A cautious, meticulous two-minute walk later, his nostrils felt the first attack on their senses. An odious stench of human feces and rot permeated around him like an invisible fence preventing anyone from coming inside what he began to see as a clearing.

"Is someone there? Help!" The sobs again punctuated the plea, this time growing in boldness as the voice sensed someone had approached.

Squinting his eyes, Faustin still could not see anyone in the clearing. Step by cautious step, he exited the protection of the wood's canopy. Scanning ahead he almost missed the pit. It was the new wave of rot and death, this time he was confident it was the imminent odor of death, that caused him to stop before entering the chasm himself. It was at least three share taxi's deep and four wide. The stench pummeled Faustin, pushing him back a step into a fallen tree branch. The branch snapped.

"Hello? Hello? Help!! Help me, please! I'm still alive! Please!"

Clarity. A killing field. Tutsi's set in a common grave.

Faustin turned and began moving as quickly as he could out of the clearing and back to the woods, back to his previous path. This time with reckless haste, he felt a thorn bush catch his shirt and reach flesh. Continuing forward Faustin felt the thorns dig deeper before their final release of their hostage. Panting he looked back at the clearing, the place Tutsi bodies were impounded, where the voice began again to sob. He fell to his knees and recognized he was by his briefcase. As he rose, Faustin determined to turn back and make his descent to his apartment. Then a very faint cry reached him, "Please. If not me then my baby."

4

Faustin put a swath of his handkerchief on his laceration and then a piece of tape to hold the makeshift bandage. Then he washed the blood as best he could from his shirt and pants. He would patch the shirt tomorrow, but would never be able to wear it to work again. Right now, he needed to sleep. He laid in his bed, not even bothering climb under his sheet. His eyes closed, and he slept. He slept, and his only dream was of that cockroach returning to his family in the wall, telling them of his near peril.

5

Exiting his regular share taxi the next morning, he saw Hutu soldiers on the taxi lane where passengers loaded. They were pulling everyone off the share taxi that followed his route the evening before. Faustin thought he saw the man who had spoken to the woman on the bus but averted his gaze before the man might recognize him in return. Walking toward his office, Faustin heard them asking about a Tutsi woman and her daughter. One officer was yelling at the driver who was trying to explain he was not working the night before. These were dangerous days.

6

At lunch, Faustin realized he had not packed a sandwich in his briefcase. Hungry, he rose from his desk and left for the grocery shop on the bottom floor. He set some crackers and hard cheese in a basket along with a pad of butter and a bread roll. He would keep what he did not eat at his desk and carry home in his briefcase. There was a subtle whisper in the back of his mind that he was buying too much food for another reason but Faustin ignored the mental muttering. Paying for the basket and a water he stepped out on the front stoop where he saw Jean-Bosco eating. Faustin sat near his officemate and opened his package of crackers. As he pulled the cheese out of his bag, he realized he had no way of cutting it or spreading the pad of butter. Jean-Bosco saw Faustin's face fall and extended his knife handle first. "Here you go."

"Thank you."

"Looks like you had a rough night? Staying late again?"

"Yes," Faustin replied. "So much to do." Faustin was thankful for his habit of staying over was an assumed reason for his current lethargy.

Jean-Bosco nodded and then looked to Faustin's market bag, "Forget your lunch?"

Another assumption as Faustin always brought lunch. "Yes. And you?"

"No. Rode the share taxi this morning. Soldiers dumped my lunch out. Said they were looking for a Tutsi woman and a kid. Not sure if they thought I was hiding her in my lunch bag," Jean-Bosco chuckled, "but you know... you can't argue."

"These are dangerous days," Faustin replied.

"Yes, they are. I figure if that lady made it out of town, she is gone. You know lots of those people are scurrying across the borders or hiding in the crawl spaces of people's homes."

"Like cockroaches," Faustin thought. He had heard the term used by soldiers describing the Tutsis. He nodded to Jean-Bosco. "Dangerous days."

7

Looking at the ever-growing stack in front of him, Faustin recognized he had spent six hours and was still working on the same two documents. His outgoing box usually full had one and only one document ready. He knew staying over would not render any better results, so he prepped to leave. He closed his briefcase after confirming the extra food was there. Perhaps he should just leave it on his desk rather than carry it back and forth? No, best to keep it with him. A few work papers he knew he wouldn't do anything with were put in, and the briefcase was shut without further rumination.

Exiting, Faustin walked by several empty desks. Reflecting on Jean-Bosco's "those people," Faustin thought about the staff members, co-workers, friends who were gone and their desks remained with their last day of unfinished work a memorial. "Those people" had been just "people" a month ago. Before the assassination, before the killings, before the dangerous days. "Those people." Those not already dead were running. Where too Faustin could only imagine.

Faustin's mind continued to spin. He hardly recognized it when he passed his share taxi loading area and returned to the area he had taken the night before. The one that would lead him to a walk through the woods.

8

Faustin exited the share taxi and stopped by a nearby food cart. These peddlers were one of the few groups who seem to have not been affected at all by the last few days. He picked up some cookies and drank a coke. He drank slowly, watching the few others who might venture through the woodland path. Once satisfied he would not find himself with unwanted accompaniment on the trail, he returned the glass coke bottle to the vendor and purchases a one-liter water to take with him.

An odd thought crossed his mind that this purchase, not the other small decisions made this afternoon, sealed his decision. The food perhaps was simple leftovers, the different share taxi a whim, but the water was intentional. Faustin entered the trailhead. A bit earlier in the evening than yesterday, he was able to recognize the tracks of the heavy machinery that had excavated the hastily formed burial hollows. Faustin could see today how they differentiated from the footpath. Coming to the primary path of the machinery, he stepped off the path toward the pits.

The smell again browbeat his senses. It was almost enough for him to turn and go back home. These were, after all, dangerous days. The smart thing was to keep to yourself and not be involved with "those people." "those people..." "people..."

Approaching the pit's edge, he lowered himself to his stomach. He took his handkerchief out of his pocket and covered his mouth as he scrutinized the hole. It was dark. The light was dimmer for the evening now approached, but there was a different kind of dark here as well. A dark made from rampant of death and decay. A darkness made from the feral wickedness that crafted this place.

"Hello?" Faustin spoke quietly. Almost as if not to be heard.

"Anyone in there?"

9

Her name was Uwimana. She and her newborn son had been there for four days. She ran out of breast milk yesterday, and her son had stopped whimpering. She had spent her day placing her ear near his mouth to feel his breath in fear his spirit would leave. She drank the water in sips, ate, and cried. Faustin asked a few questions, but all he received were her waterless tears and her murakoze, her thank you.

10

The next morning he left early. He carried his pantry's food and two 1 liter bottles in his briefcase. The trip was much more arduous uphill. Faustin stopped twice to catch his breath and also to make sure he was alone. Reaching the pathway of the heavy equipment, he turned to traverse the flatter ground and caught speed. As he crested the small rise, humanmade by the large backhoes that had dug these killing fields, he heard himself say with winded breath, "Uwimana! Uwiman..."

About to speak again, he dropped his briefcase and placed his hand over his mouth. Near the edge of the pit were two Hutu workers. "If they didn't hear you yelling, they will surely have seen you. Stupid. Stupid. Stupid. Faustin. You know better."

What he did not say was, "What are you even doing here."

Faustin collected his fallen briefcase noting that the bottom edge was damp. "Dang. One of the bottles must be leaking." He stepped into the woods and down the rise. In his haste, he felt the makeshift bandage fall from his skin under the shirt. A swift glance confirmed the wound was again bleeding. He untucked the shirt and wiped the new flow with his finger. A new flow began before he could resolve the red stain upon his current finger. It was not a harmful cut. It was not deep, but it would ruin the shirt.

Thinking again of the two soldiers, Faustin lowered himself to the ground behind a fallen tree. Opening the briefcase, he saw his few work papers were wet. The bottles were full, but one top had come loose. He did his best to fasten the top securely and re-latched the briefcase.

Now to wait. And to hope. Hope they did not see him. Hope Uwimana and the baby are ok. Hope the workers leave. Hope his absence at work will go unnoticed. Hope whatever he was feeling, this belief that somehow he has to help, is meant to help, isn't a mistake. These are indeed dangerous days.

11

The backfire of the old Suzuki Jimmy jeep was at the same time terrifying and celebration. A few seconds later, he heard the tires drive down the path he had recently trekked. Faustin's mouth tasted the dust cloud as it settled in the Jimmy's wake. Cautiously, Faustin rose from his position and saw the pit was clear of people.

This time with greater caution, he approached the opening, "Uwimana?"

"Oh, murakoze. Murakoze. I had thought you were in trouble when I heard your voice and then those men..."

Her voice faded into silence, but the fact resonated that she knew his voice, was listening for his voice. He could not remember his voice ever mattering to someone before. A smile crossed his face, and he realized it had been a long time, perhaps weeks, since he had felt those muscles stretch.

"I brought you some water and food. I'm sorry, it was only what I had in my home. I am a bachelor." Faustin lowered the bottles as far as his hand would reach then let go for them to drop to Uwimana. Then he did the same with the food.

"Please, help me out of here. I'm down here with so much... so much...."

"...death" is what Faustin knew she wanted to say. But he also knew she was on a razor's edge of sanity. Standing on corpses in a dark crater holding an infant was already too much to bear. The sentence ended without its final word being vocalized.

Of course, in all his planning to bring her food, he had not thought about her greatest need to escape. She must think him a fool. He looked up for anything to reach to her. A branch from a felled tree? Maybe some line left behind by the workers?

"Help us out," she pleaded again.

"I did not bring rope," he reluctantly admitted. "Wait."

Faustin's scanning of his surrounding became frantic. Nothing looked usable. Maybe he could ask her to search below? No, he couldn't ask her to move through a sea of men and women, neighbors and friends maybe. She needed to be out of there, not immersing herself in that darkness. Then he saw it. A piece of vine sat a few meters off the clearing.

The vine was just long enough to reach her. Somehow extending it and seeing her touch the vine's tip gave him a sensation of warmth. It was forever to be in his mind the first time they held hands. But the moment was short-lived. Her tears brought him back to focus.

"I can't. My shoulder."

For the first time, he noticed her right arm was covered in a brownish-red that did not match the light green color of her blouse. Blood. Her blood. Her arm lay limp against her body. Why had he not noticed before? It was dark. He was scared. He was... a notion passed his mind that just didn't fit the situation. Culpably, he didn't notice because he was too busy being besotted with this woman he had never even truly met. He was too busy being drawn to her.

"Can you grab it with the other arm?"

"Not and hold my child while I climb."

And there it was. They could not both escape. Not in this manner.

"Umimana, do you trust me?"

"Yes," she paused, "You are kind. I do."

"I will have to leave and come back."

A moment of silence. Then another. Palpable hesitation. Finally, "Ok. Please. Hurry? I'm scared. Those men. My baby. If they hear him cry? Please. Hurry."

As Faustin opened his mouth, he searched for what to say. What words could help her have confidence? What could he say to take her fear? Oh, what he would give to provide her the feeling of being safe. To switch places with her. His freedom for hers. His mouth opened, the odor of the pit again assaulted him, and he closed his lips without responding. Resolutely he turned and began his trip.

12

Instead of moving up the hillside to the bus stop, he went again to his apartment. He would be late either way. This way, he would have just overslept but been freshly showered and have a new shirt. He showered quickly and dressed. Then he exited his apartment to the loading area, really no more thana long dirt emergency lane, for the share taxis. He thought for a moment of abandoning work altogether, buying the rope, and returning. But the shower had sobered his thinking. There would be too many questions. And where to buy rope? If soldiers saw him? Where would he take her? Not to his home in daylight. He remembered the mom and her daughter. It must be at night under cover of darkness. He would go to work. At close he would leave, find the rope, and go back at night.

The share taxi was lightly occupied and as he pulled in to work. Faustin realized it was nearing lunchtime. Maybe he could avoid walking into questions if he could get to his desk while most were at lunch. Cautiously, he entered the floor room where the multitude of desks were arranged. No pattern but rather a hodgepodge of old office furniture, miscellaneous desk chairs, and an assortment of filing cabinets filled the space. He made his way to his desk and took his seat without the few people working through lunch making any comments. His chair with its missing wheel teetered as he placed the wooden block under the foot where a wheel should have been.

Then Mr. Kayumba, his supervisor, approached. "Working through lunch Faustin?"

Does he know? Is this a test? Ben Kayumba had never been anything but kind to Faustin since he began as manager a few years before. "No sir. I did not make it in on time this morning. I will not take lunch and will stay late."

"Not too late," Ben placed a kind hand on Faustin's shoulder, "We have much work, but it is not good to be out these days late. I hear several share taxis have even stopped running at night."

"These are dangerous days," Faustin replied.

"Yes, indeed," Ben replied. "Yes, indeed."

And with that Faustin was left to his work. A few nearby employees spoke as they returned, but all seemed satisfied that he simply slept in and arrived late. Then Jean-Bosco entered the room. Yesterday's conversation still in living memory and serving as Bosco's permission to speak. Talking entangles.

"That does not seem like your character to be late Faustin?" Jean-Bosco had remarked. "Soldiers again?"

"No. Today I simply overslept."

"Well, you still look tired, my friend. If I didn't know you, I would think you were out at a singles bar!" He placed his hand on Faustin's back-patting him twice. Then he too continued to his desk. It would be the last time Faustin would ever speak to him.

13

Before close, Faustin went to the storage closet under the pretext of obtaining a broom to sweep his area. There he saw nothing that would do for rope. He closed the door and returned to his desk with the broom, made a few token strokes around his desk, and returned the broom. He had barely done any work for the second day in a row. His mind and heart were elsewhere. Was she ok? The baby? Did the men return? Where could he find rope? Should he ask someone to help him? His mind was a whirlwind and his emotions a rollercoaster. Work had to be set aside so he could keep his composure of stoicism.

Hours ticked by excruciatingly. Finally, after all had departed and darkness had fallen, he prepared to leave. Faustin gave a modicum of attention to stack the papers neatly on his desk in some semblance of order. Then he turned and left.

On the street, he walked toward the share taxi. As he did so, he stepped into Quincallerie Uninet, a hardware store. He browsed up an aisle telling a worker he was just looking. He tried to amble slowly and examine a few items here and there before coming to the rope. Once there he saw it was on a big spool. He would have to ask someone to cut it at length. There would be small talk, questions, possibly suspicion. He walked up one more aisle picking up a painter's brush and returning it to the shelf before leaving. He still needed a rope.

14

After stopping at the market for some food and another 1-liter water, he moved toward the share taxis. He had to think of something, but he also had to know if she and the baby were ok. His insides were in knots. If he could not before the share taxi arrived, he would take her the food and water, return to his apartment, and find a solution there.

On the ride, he went through his mind to every store and vendor he could remember. It was not his routine stop, and perhaps he forgot something. Maybe there was a place? But where? Nothing came to mind.

The stop before his own the share taxi pulled in to a small loading lane off the road. Two RPF soldiers stepped into the share taxi. Faustin's heart began pounding as they scanned the seats. He knew in his mind that there was no way of them knowing his destination, but what if they began asking questions? What if they knew this was the wrong share taxi for his daily commute? It was late, and these were dangerous days."

The soldiers pointed at the three people in the front bench seat. "Move back," one ordered. The three quickly shifted to the back of the Toyota minibus. Two found purchase of what little seat remained in the back two rows, pressing Faustin even closer to his neighbors. As they did, he felt the scab on his side begin to seep. The third crouched in the small aisle and held to the shoulder of what must have been his wife.

At the next stop, Faustin asked if he could exit. He stepped over his seatmate and the man in the aisle nervously stepped past the soldiers on to the roadway outside.

"You are bleeding!" his seatmate offered. "You have it on your shirt. On my shirt!"

Faustin stepped out of the share taxi. Having already paid upon entry, he began to walk away with no intention of looking back.

"Stop!" one soldier commanded, "Stop!!"

Faustin froze. His hand went to his side impulsively. There was not a lot of blood, but his shirt was certainly damp with a stain where the scab peeled away.

"Where are you going?"

He turned to address the soldier. The other remained in the share taxi.

The soldier raised his AK47 rifle. "I asked where you were going?"

"Home sir. I – I – was at work late," Faustin managed to utter while turning back to face the soldier.

"Where do you live?"

"Kanombe."

"Kanombe?"

"Yes sir." Faustin's fist tightened on his briefcase. The weight of Umimana's food seemed to double.

"This is not the right share taxi to get there. Where are you going?" Faustin stuttered.

"I asked you a question? Why are you bleeding?"

In Faustin's mind, he heard Ben Kayumba, "We have much work, but it is not good to be out these days late. I hear several share taxis have even stopped running at night."

"Sir..." Faustin stumbled.

The soldier moved his rifle subtly upward in a sign of aggression.

"Sir, Some share taxi's have stopped running at night. I take this one and walk because it is only one ride from my work. And this," Faustin gestured to his shirt, "I was caught on a thorn bush yesterday on my way home. It just reopened."

There was a momentary pause. The soldier was deciding whether to press. A share taxi behind theirs honked, saw the soldiers, and made a gesture of apology. The one in front pulled slowly back on to the road only half loaded but eager to leave the ever-intensifying scene.

The standstill was broken not by the soldier, but a cocky voice from a Toyota minibus parked a few meters ahead and off the road. The voice came from a man wearing a flat-billed cap with Monica Lewinsky's face on it. His share taxi was exorbitantly decorated. All of them were decorated, but this one was excessive. It had "The Lewinsky" written largely down the side with a caricature of Bill Clinton blowing kisses. Bill had his pants down, butt showing, and turning his head to flash a big thumbs up. It was perhaps the funniest share taxi art Faustin had seen. Looking at the soldier, Faustin believed he thought so as well.

The Lewinsky's owner asserted, "He is right sir. I park my share taxi now. It isn't safe to drive at night. The damn cockroaches come out at night. I don't want any part of that."

The soldier smiled, "That they do, don't they?" He sneered, "The Cockroaches."

And with that, the soldier turned and re-entered his share taxi. The driver, realizing motion was in his best interest, pulled away as soon as the soldier was seated.

Faustin realized he had not breathed. A gasp came from his pursed lips. A bead of sweat trickled from his eyebrow down his cheek. "Murakoze, sir."

"Those damn soldiers are just kids. They are told to save bullets by using hatchets to kill people that use to teach them, sell them groceries, and hold them on their laps in my taxi."

He patted the Toyota minibus's side just beside Bill's backside, "I think they are strung too tight, about to snap from what they have been told to do. Most are willing to take any semi-good reason not to put more blood on their hands."

"Thank you none the less."

"Is your story true? You really make that walk through the woods?"

"Yes."

"You know there are..." the driver paused, searching for words to describe the killing fields, the pits, the darkness that resides so near their present location.

"These are dangerous days," Faustin offered.

The driver seemed relieved that his sentence would never have to be finished. "Yes, they are. I hope you are heading straight home?"

Faustin looked at the driver. If there were anyone he could ask and not fear them telling the RPF Faustin thought it would be Mr. Monica Lewensky. "Well," Faustin said, "I am after I figure out where to buy a rope."

He waited for the driver to inquire, but Mr. Monica Lewensky only smiled. Faustin's gaze went from the man's eyes to his finger-pointing and then to the top of The Lewensky's roof.

A set of wood planks were on top attached by a length of rope. A good length. Long enough to tie to a woman's waist and pull her from a pit.

"Sir?"

"Yes."

"That rope? Is any of it for sale? Ummm... There is a... ummm.. there is a part of the trail... on my way home...."

The driver looked at Faustin intently. First, he set his gaze on Faustin's eyes, checking his demeanor. Then he slowly moved to the troublesome thorn cut that shown bright red on his shirt. Then Mr. Monica Lewensky returned to Faustin's eyes. "Well, I suppose they don't call it a share taxi for nothing. How much rope do you need?"

"All of it?" Faustin asked timidly.

"All of it?" Again, that intensive look. Faustin knew he was being searched and weighed. "That is a lot of rope to carry for a bit of difficult trail?"

Faustin began, "Well, there is..."

"No matter. I can put the lumber in my taxi. I'm done for the day. Take the rope."

"How much sir?"

"Best there be no transaction. As you say, these are dangerous days." The driver smiled.

"Murakoze sir. My name is..."

"There should be no need for that detail either," the man interrupted.

Faustin nodded with the understanding that this gentleman knew more than he would say but was a friend. Faustin helped him in silence take down the five sticks of lumber and place them in the share taxi under the bench seats. He then coiled the rope and began his way.

As he walked away, the driver spoke a final word. It was a whispered voice though the message carried with clarity to Faustin's ears across the now still roadway stop. "Sir. If you should find the need. I do take one nighttime trip on Fridays. It is nonstop to Uganda. I will leave from here. Same time. Should you need such."

15

There was no answer at the pit when Faustin arrived and called her name. Faustin's heart was beating fast. He looked around to see if he was in ambush. Nothing. Darkness. The smell of death and rot. And no sound from his Uwimana. "Uwimana! Uwimana! Uwimana!!"

With each proclamation of her name and ensuing silence, he became louder, bolder, less cautious. "Uwimana!! Please! Answer!" Then he heard himself, "I can't! I can't!"

I can't what? Live without you? Ridiculous. He has never even seen her truly, never seen her out of the darkness. And yet, he knew that was exactly what his heart was saying.

Faustin began looking for something to fasten the rope to so he could descend, even at risk of being trapped himself. He would go down and find her. He must find her. And he prayed she would be alive.

As he was looking to tether the rope, he heard, "Faustin? Faustin?"

"YES! Yes! Uwimana! It is I!"

He saw her stir. A hand placed to her lips. "Shhh..."

"Yes," he reduced his voice to a whisper. "Are you alright? Your child?"

"I am weak."

"Can you loop the rope? Hold your child?"

"I must, mustn't I?"

"I fear so... my love."

The words hung. Faustin felt them go out, enter the abyss, reach the bottom, and settle on Uwimana. There was no regret. They were his words, and he meant them.

"Murakoze."

Faustin began tying a loop in each end. One for his waist and one for hers.

"Faustin?"

He would get her to place the loop around her.

"Yes, Uwimana?"

He would pull using all his might to hoist her and child up the pit's wall.

"Is it odd?"

He knew he would struggle, fall, grasp for traction.

"Is what odd?"

He would expend himself in the effort more so than any work he had ever engaged in his sedentary lifestyle.

"Is it odd that I love you too."

But he would raise her from this place, from the prospect of certain death. She would walk again but next time in his arms.   And together they would find less dangerous days.

1874: The Year of the Locust

Monica looked to the east. There was a moving gray screen backlit by the sun. She placed her bucket in the stream, drew water, and began her journey back to her family's country home.

What seemed like hail dropped all around her. The first to hit the bucket splashed its contents over her green cloth dress. The second was forceful enough to knock the bucket from her hand. She ran.

The storm crashed around her, tearing tree limbs asunder. Approaching her home, she could hear the impact upon the metal roof. Her mother was waving for her to hurry.

Entering, she realized there were bugs crawling in her dress and blouse. In a panic, she knocked the pests out of her garments. Her dad took a broom to beat the invaders. Then he returned to his project boarding up the cottage's three windows. Her mom continued to cook the stew for dinner.

An hour later, the thumping stopped. Monica's family cracked the door to see the damage. The sky was still a gray hue. Locusts piled three feet high along the fence. They covered the family's small subsistence crop. Monica looked from the crop to her pa. They all knew their food supply was gone.

Monica turned her attention to the field. She heard a desperate cry as a cow went from a vertical to a horizontal position. It was covered in locusts. The sun struggled to find paths through the swarm. The beams of light landed on the wings of the locusts transforming the dark pestilence into glistening snowflakes. The snowdrift landed on the leaning tree near their home. The combined weight of the swarm toppled the tree.

Pa ushered them in and shut the door. The family began stomping out the pests. The chimney had become an entry point. Paw worked to stuff anything movable into the opening. Several locusts attached to Monica's green skirt. She watched as the skirt dissolved under their veracious appetite. In a moment she, and her family, were nearly naked. They all had bite marks over their body. Their blankets, baskets, and rug were in ruin. Destruction and death became an audible hum around the family.

Pa exited the home again. He had constructed a crude torch from a plank of wood soaked in lamp oil. Monica waited inside the home. She held her baby sister. She wanted to tell her it would be alright, but was not sure she could. There was a bright flash of light. The fire was started.

Pa entered the home and motioned for everyone to follow. Outside, the fallen tree burned, creating a small window of protection for the family to move to the tornado shelter. As Monica ran past the burning tree, she saw the locusts were dousing the flames by their sheer numbers.

In the tornado shelter, maw tended paw's injuries. Then, they sat in darkness. A day went by, then a week. Provisions expended, the family surfaced. They stood in a field of corpses. The locusts had taken everything and left only death behind. Monica looked to the east. A single ray of light shown, illuminating the apocalyptic landscape.

In the Mind

We have to get going. We need to make the bed for sure.

We have time. They won't be up for another hour.

Unless they came in last night and changed the clock?

Who does that? That would be mean.

The bed is wet. Did we pee the bed?

No, of course, we didn't. It is wet by the pillows. Someone spilled water.

They will be sooooo mad! Come over here to the trash can. We left all sorts of clothes out too.

I don't understand? Some of these clothes-

You fool, I have said it over and over. This is not our room. These are the clothes a teenager would wear. I mean, underwear with tacos on it and a Rolling Stone t-shirt?

Then whose room is it?

Their kid. He is like seventeen.

Where is he?

I mean, look at these shirts with "Ridgeline High School" on them? They are for a child. We don't go to school.

Why are they all over the floor?

I don't know. Maybe he didn't clean up before we got here?

Or maybe he came in last night. Perhaps he was watching us sleep?

Don't be ridiculous. Why would a seven-year-old watch us?

Maybe they sent him. Maybe he put devices in the drawers? Perhaps we are being watched right now?

I think we may have thrown them there.

We really need to stop worrying about the clothes. We have to fix this water problem. What if it wasn't an accident and there is a leak?

On the bed?

We don't know. That is the point. Let's get the cover over the wet spot.

The cover is wet too. And, look, there is a phone here?

We poured the water there. You wanted to keep the phone from tracking us. We poured the water on it. Didn't want to move the phone, so brought the water here in a cup.

If so, where is the cup?

Let's go check the bathroom. If there is a cup, it will be in there.

What do you see?

There is a cup in here. It is wet inside. It has been used recently.

By us. See?

But look at this. There is Suave shampoo. We don't ever use commercialized shampoo. The additives make you groggy. Someone else has been in here.

Idiot. You are a freaking idiot. I told you already. This is not our room. It is a boy's room. We just came to stay the night.

Then why does the pill bottle have our name on it?

We can't take those pills. They make us feel blind. We can't see the world clearly on those. We have to get out of here before they make us take them.

After we make the bed. You should always make the bed first.

The pill bottle has our name on it. But so does the picture frame.

Let me look. "Our boy. Charles." That could be a coincidence.

I don't like it here. It isn't safe being inside like this. Too easy to find us.

That is the first sensible thing you've said. Let's get this bed made. And we will put a note on the nightstand. "Sorry, we spilled the water."

Okay. But write it left-handed so it won't look like our writing.

Do you see the notebook next to the pad of paper? Pictures. These are pictures of us! As a young kid, a teenager. Look, here is one that looks almost exactly like the person we just saw in the mirror.

Do you think it is a one-way mirror? I didn't consider that. I'm scared.

Look, the bed is made. We put the clothes that weren't ours in the pillowcases and folded the openings down so they won't come out again. Let's go.

What about the pictures? I think this is our bedroom. Our parents' house, maybe.

Nonsense. If it was our parents' house, we would have our own room. We wouldn't share it with some teen boy.

Unless we were that boy? What if that medicine? What if our parents will walk through that door? Then we would know this is our place? And it would be safe?

The only safe place is on the streets. Keep moving. That's how to keep them from finding you. Look, I packed our stuff. I took the Brown Sugar

Pop-Tarts the kid left. Two whole boxes. Can we leave him something in payment?

All I have are a few buttons.

Leave a green one and two blue ones. That should do. Do you all mind if we leave through the window? I want to avoid any cameras that might be on the front door.

So you all don't want to stay and see if it is our parents? What if we are sick? What if we need help? What if-

I do the worrying for us. And I say better to leave. We can find a hiding spot and watch the house a bit from a distance. See who comes and goes. Carefully, of course. Someone might try and follow us.

That's a good idea. Did you take the battery out of the phone?

I don't think it is ours. Besides, it has water all over it.

Leave it here, then. Let's go.

Bye, mom. Bye, Dad. I love you, and we tried.

Roll of the Dice

First off, just because I'm quiet doesn't mean I don't see nothing. In fact, might mean I see more. Like on this deck for instance. Man wants the old one torn out. A new one the same dimensions put back. He doesn't want to restore it none. Probably same with his wives. One in his living room is wearing a big diamond ring, too much lipstick for lounging around the house, and a skirt so short it is hard to tell where the middle is. As for the man, well, anyone would notice pretty quick he was likely out of high school when his wife was born. Odds are, there once was another wife, one his age. Like this deck, he decided it was time to replace it.

As for me, I'm in recovery. I want to rebuild, not replace.

My crew were up and running. Good crew is like that. Once you get them situated, they don't really need you. Good thing too. Allows me to go set up their next paycheck. There's always the missing board or the extra pack of fasteners. They'll call me and let me know. I'll get it to them. "Boss man has to look busy," they'll say. But they all know I put them first. Everyone in recovery has a "I got clean because…" I ain't married no more. No kids. Parents gone. My "what for" is these guys. They hitched their wagon as the saying goes to me and I'm their ticket to a better life. One deck, one sheetrock wall, one roof truss at a time.

But my crew, they are top notch. All three of them. Family men. They are even learning some English. Which is good. Usually, it's the kids who learn it fastest. Then the moms and the dads last. I push mine to use English whenever they can. Best way to go home and not feel like you worked all day just to see your kid jabbering on about something you know nothing about. Living like that I figure is like when I wa on drugs. See what's going on around you but you are lost in it all. I don't want that for them. I want better. Someone who works as hard as they do in the game of life deserves to feel like they are winning.

That includes my fourth guy, Juan. I can't give guys insurance. No way. My buddy wants to make it all political, but I say it doesn't matter who made the situation. Just have to deal the cards dealt. And when Juan fell off the roof a few weeks ago and shattered his leg, he was dealt a bum one. I've been giving him his pay still. It is tough since we are a man down, but my other guys stepped up. Good crew.

They don't call me Gringo, though I look it. My Spanish came honest from my mom's side. Dad went to Mexico for a vacation one year. One of them all-inclusives. Apparently, he thought all-inclusive meant wives also because he came back with one. She got citizenship, and later my granma and uncles.

It was a full house. My dad put money in the bank and Momma put a hot meal on the table every day, clean clothes, and gave him me and my brother. They were as close as I ever seen to soul mates. It didn't just happen. People think that's the way it is. It isn't. They made it work, day in and day out. Little by little. When I came along a few years later they had their first house. My dad taught me and my brother construction remodeling it. Suppose I fell in love with swinging a hammer like my dad. But it was Momma who taught me how to run a business. Momma taught me how to see the little things. Like how a little jalepeno can change a dish, or how an honest price brought you more customers and an unfair price brought you a bad reputation, or how a man holds his shoulders can tell you whether he's honest. She always said my dad had good shoulders. He'd joke that her salsa was too hot and she didn't charge enough when she cooked for neighbors. It was all in fun, though. She'd rub his shoulders and laugh. Then tell him to take some extra food to his crew.

I pulled into the road after my Maps told me to take a right "and your destination will be on your left." Crazy thing, how it knows not only where I am but where I'm going. Most people don't know both. Maybe one, but not both. Like this man I'm meeting, for instance.

"Eric?" he asked. His left shoulder leaned lower than his right. Momma would say watch out for such men. Their money is crooked. But in the remodel business sometimes you gotta take crooked money in a straight line to the bank.

"Yes sir." It is really Enrique, But that just confuses people, when they see I look white. I stuck out my hand. He gave a pillowy hand shake. It was soft. Professional, yes. But soft. Not the handshake I expected on this street. Not the kind of handshake for a run-down, dead-end road lined with old, dilapidated double wides. I looked around. You could see five houses from the porch of this one. The one next door looked the newest. That said, it still was bult some three or four presidents ago. On the other side of this place there were two lots visible. One a single wide trailer set back off the road and the other an RV that probably hadn't seen a road since the day it mistakenly pulled into its driveway. Ironically, it looked the nicest with the warm glow of cheap Christmas lights dangling from its still intact awning. The two across the street looked every bit of forty years. In the first apparently lived a man who worked on small engines. Mowers, golf carts, a few chainsaws and weed eaters populated his front yard under three of those metal frame carports. The other seemed to have a lawn gnome in the yard for each year the occupants had lived there. They all looked tattered and worn. Not just old, but neglected. Their roof confirmed the story with three tarps layered on top of each other over one side. An elderly couple sat on the porch smoking. A fallen gutter downspout still in the yard, a crushed chain link fence with a portion of a rotting tree laying on each side, and a barking chihuahua completed the image.

I took a moment to examine the home that Maps brought me too. This house had a modified porch built around a chimney. The chimney had three or four different color bricks. Whoever built this add-on to an old double wide, probably called a "manufactured home" when it was produced, really wanted a traditional fireplace. My guess was inside there was a hearth and everything. A place to hang stockings at Christmas and set easter baskets in the spring. It looked like after cutting the wall and putting in the insert, they just acquired bricks from wherever they could. A patchwork lot of discards ran up the side of the home. Life can be like that. Sometimes we have no plan. Some people have a meticulous plan. Some of us just have ten or fifteen different plans, like different color bricks, that patch together to make a life. I immediately liked this old chimney and the man who once built it. I knew it wasn't the pillowy handshake of a man in front of me.

The chimney stopped two feet short of where it should've. Whoever took on this project never finished. The cheap plywood wheelchair ramp set over a nice cedar deck confirmed that the home's builder was gone and the newest owner did not take the same care. Indeed, he probably had a pillowy hand-shake and a crooked shoulder. In the yard was a "For sale by owner" sign.

"I'm Levi. This is my folk's place," the man said. "George died fifteen or so years ago. Lilly wouldn't leave it."

I admit I was a bit confused. When I'm confused my jaw drops a bit. My mom always said it was my tell. While I thought the man had a slumped left shoulder and all, I didn't think him the type to marginalize his mom and dad by only using their first names. That's disrespect on a whole other level.

He apparently didn't notice my jaw drop or didn't care. He continued. "I Told her I had enough money to put her somewhere nice. She just wouldn't do it, you know." He waited for me to nod, agreeing that this place wasn't nice and that he had the money. I gave him the nod. Not because those two things were true, but because this house had more love and care than this thirty-something would ever understand. I nodded for George and Lilly.

"This is nice cedar,' I said to let him know the pause was long enough. "Don't see cedar decks anymore."

"Yeah, George built it. He loved this old piece of crap. Came home most days and worked the yard or something."

"Was it his job? Working with wood? It is a fine deck."

"No, he worked a factory or something. But built most of the things around here." The man's arm swung wide to point to two sheds out behind the home and a still useful privacy fence, though a few of the individual boards had given way to age and gravity. "I had to add this ramp on it three years ago. Lilly got to where she couldn't do stairs anymore. And like I said, she just wouldn't let me take care of her."

Another pause to reflect on the only care he could offer was to pay for someone else to do it. I nodded. It was probably true. Certainly, if he built this ramp it was. The ramp looked like the kind of thing my crew would laugh at before tearing it out.

He motioned me inside. I was expecting the cheap, vintage cabinets of a late seventies home, maybe a dark green countertop and some sort of wallpaper with cowboy boots or sunflowers. What I saw were exquisite cabinets. Lower doors were removed and showed signs of wheelchair marks. There was an aging parquet flooring, and the ceiling told the story that whoever sat in the left recliner was a heavy smoker. Along the hallway was an inset bookcase filled with National Geographics and Time Magazines.

"I know, the place looks horrible. Lilly was a bit of a hoarder. Never would let those figurines go in the curio cabinet. Didn't care that the cabinet there blocked part of both bedroom doorways. But we will get that out. Got someone coming to take it all to auction."

"You raised here?" I knew it wasn't wise to get too personal with a client. This questions skirted the line. He could answer superficially or dive deep into his memories of the place.

"Yeah... well, sort of. I grew up over there." He pointed in the direction of the house filled with lawn mowers. "My real dad went to prison and my mom couldn't stay off the needle. So they brought me in. It was good of them, I guess. But I got in to college and into banking."

Another pause. This one for me to fill in the "...and out of here."

"This way," he motioned. As we went to the side of the home away from the curio cabinet blocking doorways he casually pointed to the walls and ceiling. "Want you to quote me on painting all this. Fresh coat of paint probably do it good for retail value. Though I can't imagine getting much for it no matter what in this neighborhood. But if its cheap enough..." He paused in the doorway to the master bedroom, pointing a finger at me. "And that's key. I want to do the least amount possible to get this up to market. Nothing more."

I nodded and we entered the master bedroom. The room was larger than I would've expected. There was several old dressers. My guess is they were bought when the house was. They were certainly made of real wood, not that glued pressboard stuff sold today. The bed was a Queen. It was clear that one side sagged more than the other. The side with medicine bottles and a can of Aquanet. The other side had a clean nightstand with nothing on it but a small clock and a hat. The hat read, "Alston. We make the games you play."

He must've seen my gaze. "George's old hat. Alston. That's the name of it. He worked at Alston. You know, that factory downtown that makes board games. Life, Monopoly, Candyland... what's the other... oh yeah, Hi Ho Cherry-o"

"I loved those games," I offered.

"Paid my college I guess." Then he pointed at the floor. "Right there, under the rug. There's a metal plate or something. Where Lilly's wheelchair turned and spun."

I stepped gingerly on the identified area. If she had been wheel chair bound for three years, it didn't make sense there would be a hole in the floor. Took a lot more wear and tear than that, especially a house like this. Manufactured home or not, it had pretty good bones. I pulled up the rug. When I did, a large stop sign appeared.

"Well, I'll be. Old man put a stop sign over the floor. Crazy."

The sign heavy, but I found a gap to get my fingers under and pried it up. There was a hole in the floor where the middle of the stop sign stood. I thought George must've been a clever man to repurpose an old sign. That or there were a lot of accidents on some nearby street. I looked up. It seemed to me the man who refused to call these two his parents had no idea about the stop sign till just now. He probably never thought to look. Then I remembered that his left shoulder slumped just a bit more than the right. It wasn't he didn't think to look, he just didn't care too. That kind of work was for lesser people. Perhaps people like George and Lilly. People like me.

My cell phone buzzed twice. I answered and my crew was stopping for lunch. They needed some Thompson water seal after. I hung up. The man seemed annoyed I had taken a call. "That was my crew. Finishing a job."

"How much." We were all business now.

I pondered the job. $35 for the plywood. A couple bucks for a 2x4. Plus the labor. "I can fix the hole – assuming there are no suprises – for $150. Can paint the living room for another $200."

"Just the hole. I'll get back to you on the living room. Might come down and do it myself Saturday."

He wouldn't. He would call me and tell me rather than ask just as we finished the job. But that's okay. My momma taught me to read people and situations. I would pay my guys for each job separately, even though I wouldn't see a dime till we finished painting.

"When can you get it done."

"It's Thursday. I can get started on Monday." I actually had a siding job in front of this one, but the weather was coming in. Nothing but rain next week. This would be a good filler till the next project dried up. He agreed after a short protest that he wished I could do it tomorrow. Then we shook on the deal. He warned me again not to do more. And if I got into that hole and it was more than $150, just leave it and he'd sell the place as is.

We shook, though I'm not sure his handshake meant too much. So I went ahead and wrote out a fast contract. He signed and I did too. Gave him a copy and headed to the hardware store for sealer.

Next Monday my crew and I pulled up into the driveway. Note on the door said, "Neighbors have the key. House with gnomes in the yard."

They were on the porch and I came over. "Good morning," I offered.

"You must be the company here to fix George and Lilly's place?"

"Yes, ma'am." The lady set down a half smoked ciggarret. With difficulty, she stood and reached for her walking stick. Getting her feet under her, she stepped inside her sliding glass door. A moment later she emerged dangling a key.

"Good people, George and Lilly." She paused waiting for me to agree. Perhaps if I didn't she was going to withhold the key. I nodded, though. Her shoulders were hunched over with age, but you could see they once sat straight. These were good people.

"You knew them well," I offered as I reached for the keys.

"Moved in a few weeks after they did. This whole area was owned by a farmer. Sold off the property in pieces and we all snatched it up. Good people on this street."

"Well, except for the next door neighbor," her husband offered. "I mean, guy there now is fine. But before...."

He trailed off his sentence as if I should know what "before" meant. I think my jaw must've dropped. His wife added, "He mean's the family there years ago. Was the farmer's son. He moved to the city. Got hooked on some awful things. Came back here with a pregnant girlfriend, an expensive habit, and-"

"And a series of dumb decisions his dad eventually couldn't cover up."

I looked back at George and Lilly's place and then to the home next door with lawn equipment strewn everywhere. "Their kid, that's who hired me, I think. Believe George and lilly adopted him?"

I left the pause in the air. It was the woman who took it up. "They did. Couldn't find nicer people. Boy's dad robbed Richard's Quick Mart a few blocks away. Richard pulled a shotgun out and the two had a shootout. Richard took the worst of it with a shot to the chest, but the boy's dad took a life sentence for robbery and murder. His mom was just barely functional even then. But a few weeks later, she had some new guy over. Two of them caught the house on fire while high. It was George that went in and drug them out. The boy too. After that, George brought the boy to their home."

"I knew he was a good man," I offered. "See it in the craftsmanship of his chimney and deck." I paused before adding, "And can see it in you too." I pointed to the deck we were standing on.

"This thing? It is falling apart."

It was, but even old things falling apart can tell you they were once grand. Probably should've told them that, but didn't. I hope they already knew it. I think they did, at least based on his wife's next comment.

His wife lit a cigarette with the stub of the previous one. "It is now. We are too old and no kids of our own. But you are right. In our day, we kept this place looking nice."

"When I'm done with George and Lilly's place, let me come over and price you out some work. Wouldn't take much."

"We ain't got much, I'm afraid," She said. "Last guy we had quote it was way more than we could do."

"I'm honest and will quote you fair. You seem like good people." With that I turned. My crew were waiting on the porch. Hosea was jumping up and down on the wheelchair ramp, laughing at how flimsy it was.

A few moments later we had the rug and stop sign up. We cut the hole into a straight square and began prepping some braces to hold a new sheet of plywood. It was then that Mario found the box.

He pulled it out from under the house, using the rope attached to it anchor bolted to the plywood we just cut up. We opened it. Inside was a small cash box and two smaller wooden boxes. One held one of those label printer labels saying, "Magic Marbles" and the other had hand-painted on the front "Lighthouses and Seahorses."

"What is this jefe?" Mario asked.

"Not sure, but it is for the owner to decide." With that, I set it on the bed and we finished the patch job. Sure enough, as we were packing up the man called. He was unable to get out there that past Saturday and needed us to go ahead and paint. He asked me if I'd take less money. I said, "No," and he harrumphed before telling me to get started.

That afternoon he arrived. He asked me how much to tear out the wheelchair ramp and finish up the chimney. I told him I'd have to give him the quote after looking it over, but first needed to show him the box.

He opened it with a banker's curiosity moreso than a child whose life was saved by a kind couple. He jiggled the cash box, finally prying it open with a kitchen knife. He gave a hoot of joy as he pulled out three stacks of hundreds. I didn't count with him. Such things are not how my Momma and dad taught me, but it had to be ten thousand in total.

"Silly folks," he muttered. Never trusted banks." Then looking at me, "You aren't going to cheat me on that price now, are you? Now that you know I got this?"

"No sir," I said and meant it. I figured prices based on cost of labor and materials, not mystery boxes under a house. A few minutes later I tallied up the project and gave him the total.

"Sounds good. Just do it," he said. Then with a smirk, "And I'll pay in cash."

As he walked away, I gathered my moxy. That's what my momma used to call it anyway. "Sir, the game. If you don't want it, can I have it? Me and my kids we love a good-"

"Yeah, yeah," he interrupted.

"Both of them?"

"Any you find in the house." Then he turned and pointed a finger at me. "But if you find any more money, that comes to me."

There were three more found in the chimney. Each with a stack of hundreds. Five board games in total. My crew and I finished the work. I paid them out of my account. Then I waited for Levi to swing back by. When he did, it was clear he was already several beers in.

I presented the contract for work completed. He started to sign and then realized he didn't have a pen on him.I went back to my truck and grabbed one. As I reached over the console and saw the stack of games, I paused. I looked up over my dash and took a quick inventory of the man, He stood there, shoulders slumped. He had his stack of hundreds out, thumbing through them like they were treasured pictures on his phone. And he had new sunglasses. Might as well had the tag still dangling. I smiled and he smiled back. New shirt, a bright purple Polo. And white shoes. I didn't know the brand, but I figured it thinned his pile of bills a good bit.

I remembered momma. A jalepeno can change everything. I took the contract back and before handing it to him wrote in the addendum notes: "Owner agreed to give me full possession to board games gathered in the home as part of payment."

"Hey, Why did you write that?"

"I just always write down any terms of agreement."

"Whatever, I got a date here I got to get to. Beer-thirty if you know what I mean." He chuckled and scribbled his name. Then counted out the cash.

He did have time to wait for me to make eight dollars change. Apparently it was just ten till beer-thirty.

I went home and poured over the games. I want bore you with the details, but before it was over I got to meet some execs at Hasbro. Juan and my guys got insurance. I still run a crew, continue to hire guys like me trying to get their feet under them in some way or another. Guys with good shoulders, strong handshakes, and eyes that say they want to be the right of this world. And yes, we went back and polished up that whole neighborhood.

As for Levi, he protested, of course. Went nowhere since I had my bill of sale and multiple witnesses. He got a little something from his parents not realizing how much more they had to give him, even in tehir death. I figure it was like that when they were alive too. I'm quiet, but I see. A man like that who just takes and takes matched up in a house with a couple who love and give is a peculiar thing. You see, love not only has to be given, it has to be received for it to work.

Bed Racing: A Covid Tale

The door slammed. Kirk looked over his recliner at his prized Red Sox autographed glove. The slammed door had vibrated its encasement to the precipice of the curio cabinet. Another shudder and the cruel mistress named gravity would shatter the glass encasement on the floor of his mancave.

Kirk rose and walked to the door. Pushing the glove back onto the shelf, he glimpsed a child, likely one of his, rush past in purple underwear and a cape. A few seconds later a second, definitely his, followed with a cereal box. Stepping into the hallway, Kirk saw the trail of Lucky Charms down the hall.

"Kirk!" came his wife's voice behind the slammed door. "Kirk!!"

"Yes, sweetie?"

"They are yours."

It took twenty minutes to locate two of his four-wheel piano dollies. Another ten to convince his neighbor John to locate his. The two men gathered the kids in the yard, six feet apart. An idea was hatched. The sport of Bed Racing was born.

The old twin box spring and mattress fit nicely on the two dollies. There were no steering wheels, but since when did seven-year-olds know how to steer anyway? That is what a bike helmet is for. And pillows. He and John agreed there should be lots of pillow.

The two race beds were rolled diligently up the neighborhood hill. His youngest, still in the cape though he had donned pants, was finishing a juice-pop. He looked every bit the part of Dale Earnheart drinking a cola before Talledega. His more cautions child had his hand down in the Lucky Charms box. Kirk hated to tell him all the marshmallows were along the hallway corridor.

John's son and daughter took their places on their respective racer.

"Lady and gentlebugs," Kirk announced.

"Dad, we aren't bugs!" Sammy said while adjusting his cape for the best wind velocity.

"Oh sorry. Lady and gentlemen! This race is to the bottom of Sleepy Hill. First bed to the curb wins the grand prize! A month supply of goldfish crackers!"

With that, the two dads pushed off. The beds twisted and turned like a carnival tilt-a-whirl. There was no reckoning to the dollie's independent decisions. John's landed him in the curb twice requiring costly foot-on-the-ground penalties. Kirk, too, had trouble as one wheel snapped midway down the hill sending the cart in a looped-de-loop. Lucky Charms and caped children were almost ejected as Kirk's bed racer crossed the chalk drawn finish line a few feet before John's.

John's daughter jumped up and down on the bed like an inflatable bouncy house. "Again! Again!"

The children were sent in to retrieve new stuffed animal passengers. Fluffy bear would help navigate and pink bunny would oversee the entourage of nerf guns being assembled. John suggested quietly water balloons. Kirk, the moderate one of the two, thought to save such escalation for the third or fourth round. He figured they could get at least two more in before either wife came outside, wondering why their house had become so quiet.

His elderly neighbor, another Red Sox lover, asked him the over-under and if there were still time to place a bet. It had been too long since real sports aired anywhere. The first neighborhood casualty to the Coronavirus had been their traditional March Madness BBQ.

Kirk redirected attention to his son. The Lucky charms had been traded for the nerf blaster 3000. John shrugged as his daughter loaded a cardboard box of stuffed bears to throw in retaliation. Bed Racing just took on a violent flare.

Four other neighborhood kids stood by wishing their dads had the vision of Bed Racing. Simon, an engineer down the street, said he would return in twenty to enter the next round. Another dad, Kirk did not know his name but quarantine brought people together like this, just strapped his kid into a bean bag chair on a dolly. The dad said he would run the rails like a hobo on a train car.

Since there were no written rules, Kirk and John allowed the entry. After all, it was day ten of the city-wide quarantine. And Kirk smiled. His boss had sent him home saying, "Stay safe at home in your bed."

Home Show

I no longer dine with my depression. I walk. Downtown. I like the cobble streets and the street lamps. Sometimes I can be Mary Poppins or Ginger Rogers. On Chestnut Street I walk by a maple tree. I love its sense of rebellion and confidence. I wish to be that.

Today the convention center is full of visitors. They view me through the eyes of their own elations. Chattanooga is new to them. My pink coat and pink hair draw their gaze and my blue umbrella evokes their smiles. Their excitement to be here settles on me like sunshine.

Today my eyes are tired. At my age, even the cold, wet paper towel in the center's bathroom does not help. Nevertheless, the lotus flower tattoo blooming into doves on my arm tell me hope exists.

Exiting the bathroom of the convention center, a man offers me a free t-shirt. It says, "Hullco Windows." If I wear it, then I can enter the Home Show for free. I like the blue hue. So many blues are sad, but this one reminds me of a Wedgewood necklace my grand wore. I touch my neck where it would have hung and almost feel her aged hands over mine.

Missing my Grand, I almost return to my dreary bedroom. The man again invites me in to the show. His invite is not necessary but appreciated. Being invited feels wonderful.

I am amazed how many ways there are to cook potatoes. A lady selling a copper pan makes potato chips. The sample is salty. My stomach has been angry with me lately, but accepts the chip skeptically. I promise it if we find someone sautéing chicken I will let it decide.

At the end of the first row is a stone worker's booth. I am Alice and step up the stone steps to a patio. An Aerodyne chair beckons me to find respite. I sit before an iron fire pit in a make-believe backyard. Someone has cut butterflies into the metal ring. The propane fire sends heat toward my feet in the shape of a monarch butterfly. Its wings warm my toes and the semicolon tattoo on my ankle.

A toddler sits beside me. He asks if this is my real hair. I tell him no and it is not my porch either. I am just pretending.

He likes to pretend. He has a stuffed giraffe. He says the giraffe likes my hair also and says, "hello." I believe him and tell the giraffe, "thank you."

I look again at my shirt. Under the window it says, "Make life a little better, come to Hullco."

At my home depression lingers, waiting with laundry, dirty dishes, and whispers of my inadequacy. It can wait. Up the next aisle I smell flowers and candles. As I rise and say goodbye to the toddler and Mr. Giraffe. My stomach settles. It agrees that if there is chicken in the next row, we will stop there too.

So You Know the Truth of It

As a kid I always loved stories about ghosts, but it wasn't till I was in prison that I ever got buried with one. Name's Kolby. And I ain't nothing special. Grew up over in Dunlap, Tennessee. Dropped out of school and took a job doing security at a country club. Really just walking around and telling ladies how pretty they looked. A good gig, in retrospect. But I was young, did some side hustle removing stumps with dynamite, and that country club had a safe. You always hear cons say, "If I could go back, I'd..." Well, I doubt I would've done it any different. Ain't bragging there, just being honest.

I was nineteen and my wife had a dream to go to college. She was always going somewhere and I mean that. I married up, if you know what I mean. She had goals and drive. I had a 1960's mustang and a minimum-wage security job. I was sure if I didn't deliver the cash for her schooling, she'd figure it out without me. She wasn't one to go through the back entrance anywhere. She was going to be a member of that club one day, marching right through the front door. And she'd do it with me if I could provide. Without me if I couldn't. So, like I was saying, if I could go back I'd likely play it out the same.

I walked around that country club opening doors, tipping my hat to the ladies, joking with the men about their golf swing, not that I ever held a golf club. The whole time, I was thinking about that safe. They ran a poker game couple nights a week. All the cash made by the house went in there. 1981 wasn't like today. That game was all cash. Off the books cash. It was three years of nursing school all tightly rubber-banded and counted.

Plan was simple enough. Wait till everyone gone, slip back in. A few cameras taken down and turned off for maintenance the day before – routine stuff back then when they recorded on VHS - and it would be easy in and easy out. One stick of dynamite and the safe would blow. Collect the money and drive away. Except I overcharged the load and the place caught fire. Probably would've still been okay except on the way in I stopped by the cig machine. Back then they had them out like vending machines. I said I wouldn't change anything, but if I could maybe I would've worn some gloves. Or at least forgone the need for a smoke. Fingerprints all over the inside area of that cigarette machine I busted up, It was a smart cop who found it in the rubble and thought to see if their arsonist had a penchant for Marlboro reds. Fingerprints were just becoming a thing, so maybe I didn't know to think about it. And maybe getting caught was for the best. Suppose if I had used gloves and gotten away with it? I might've done another job. Once you get a taste, they say you keep going back to the well. Maybe that was the Lord's way of keeping me from killing someone. Well or at least not more than one more someone.

That night anyway, no one died. Thank goodness or I'd be strapped in to Ole Sparky up in Nashville. Instead, I was sent to Pine Mountain State Penitentiary. Ten-year stretch. Now, I know. You want me to get to the part about the ghost. Hold on. First you gotta understand.

My dad was broken. His only son a convicted arsonist and thief. But he stood by me. Sure enough. Even though he had to be disgraced. He was a police officer in our hometown, after all. He convinced the court to let him escort me to Pine Mountain, himself. Took me up on his Harley one beautiful August day. Maybe it wasn't that beautiful. Maybe that's just my memory of it in light of the next few years. I recall pulling up to those two large metal doors off the side of this large prison. Prison was shaped on the hill like an upside down cross. Someone later told me that was because you were condemned soon as you walked in. Maybe so. I breathed my lasty breath of free air, hugged my dad, and stepped through those doors with Dora, one of the prison's female correctional officers. She wasn't the one who liked to watch us shower. That was Janie. Dora was okay.

That day though, she was my first taste of prison. She marched me in to a covered porch on B Block. Cage bars all around where a normal place might have screen windows. Porch stood about four feet higher than the yard where inmates lulled around. I ain't a man of many big words, but I know the word "lull" well enough. Means it gets quiet. But not just any quiet. That quiet where you know something is about to happen. Lot of lulling in the yard.

"Fresh fish!" came a voice. Followed by several whistles and a volley of "He's a pretty one." "Young as I've seen one in some time." And "hey fish, I got an empty cot. Killed my cellmate just last week. Wouldn't play the way I like. I bet you will though."

As they taunted, I was stripped naked. I thought it was to make sure I didn't have contraband or anything, but found out later Dora was just checking for lice and crabs. Hell, I didn't even know what a crab was. Didn't know much about life outside the prison. Even less about life inside prison. When that metal door slammed, it was like I was reborn into a different world. Like a newborn infant, I stood in my birthday suit. But instead of crying in front of my parents and a nurse or doctor I did it in front of my new eleven hundred closest friends. Dora had the decency to stand between me and most of them gawking in the yard as I walked by.

First two nights I slept in solitary. Not because I was doing something wrong. It was to keep me from being hurt. Like the kid who walks into the water in the shallow end rather than jumping in the deep, just in case he can't swim. They let you spend a day or two in the yard before a night in gen pop. First night in solitary I got a cheeseburger. Second night some casserole and a stale roll. Third night I went to my cell in A Block after my meal was taken in the cafeteria.

Originally A Block was white and B Block was black. By the eighties the blocks were integrated, but not the cells. My roommate was Riccardo. Not much to say on that other than he would be dead within my first year. Not by me. Only blood on my hands was someone else. I ain't bragging none. Just saying how it is.

Ain't much to tell about day-to-day life inside. It's a dangerous place. Big Red, a near seven-foot Irishman, ran the yard. He had a crew under him. If he nodded in your way, meant you were getting a beating. If he pointed, meant you'd be in the medical by nightfall or worse. If he ever pulled his finger across his throat before pointing at you, then you wouldn't make it to the med hall. There weren't no recourse. No one ever sweated an inmate going to the great beyond whether by his own hand or another's. Whether fast with a shiv or the slow fade of drugs. Both were efficient and most just assume a prisoner was closer to being dead than alive. That's probably why guards did so little to stop the drugs. Saw more dope inside than I ever did outside. Guys hiding it in shoes, eight-track cassettes, cigarette boxes, pretty much whatever could be holed out.

I stayed away from dope, but always loved a hot cup of coffee. I suppose the one thing Ricardo did for me before he died was made a prison microwave. Took a fan cord, cut it and wrapped it so wouldn't electrocute us. Plug one end into the outlet and the other in the coffee cup. Have hot water every morning. That's one nice thing he did for me. Of course, he also told Big Red my dad was a cop and I was a security guard on the outside. Thought it would save his own life, I reckon. Trade a little info for some air to breathe. It was good info too, though it didn't save him in the end. I ain't bragging or nothing. Just saying it was how it was. I might as well have been a cop myself after that got out. That info didn't just get a nod or a point. Big Red done come all the way over to me and introduced me to his buds.

"Hey fish, what's yo' name?"

"Kolby."

"Kolby. Like coal. You know this prison used to be a working coal mine. Prisoners go up in those hills every day. Had to come back each day with your quota of coal or they tied you to the whipping post. They did. Post still out there in the yard with the grate under it where all that blood drained. Guards back then would dip their leather bullies in the sand bucket we use for cigarette butts so their strikes would pull off a little extra skin when they beat you. If you died, they just chunked you in the mine shafts. No whipping in the yards these days, but those mines still open. And that grate still takes the blood whenever there is an..." Big Red leaned over as if telling me a secret. "... whenever there is an incident around here."

I knew Big Red wasn't giving me a history lesson just to build a friendship. I also had no idea how to answer. I just stood quiet.

"We still work those mines, boy. At least some and it ain't hard to get a guy switched over to that detail. Easy to get lost up there. Or maybe a guy gets hurt here in the yard and his blood flows down that grate to those mine tunnels. Sometimes warden reports such an incident to the state. Lot of paperwork there. Lot of paperwork. Much easier to just say he was working a mine and slipped into one of those mineshafts. Or tell the state he couldn't take it no more and done jumped in on purpose. No one goes up to confirm. Guy just disappears. Sure, family might ask for a body but nobody going to really look. And poof." Big Red clapped his massive hands together. It startled me as I was already on edge. "Guy just disappears. Even a copper's kid. You know what I mean?"

I did know. I knew Big Red was telling me my future. He patted me on the back hard. I coughed, trying to regain my breath as he walked away. I looked at the sun, as good a clock as anything else, and saw it was almost noon. Big Red and I just had our showdown. I was on borrowed time.

I had been in six months at that point. Knew the routine and kept my head down. I also knew the rule of the yard. Every need is a debt.

Every need a debt. Two cells down "Buick" – I never knew his real name – converted a Walkman cassette player into a tattoo gun. Cost me a pack of cigs to have my wife's name put on my arm and three packs to have him put a wolf on top of it when she told me she was divorcing my imprisoned ass. My dad put money in my commissary and sent me a six-inch TV. I paid a pack of cigs for the Rock Man to extend my unraveled Coke can from my cell block to the outside so my small TV antenna could catch channel ten. Another pack of cigs got me roof duty one day. It was nice to see over the wall, even if just two hours. Every need a debt. I had a need. I needed to make right with Big Red. This need would cost a lot more than a pack or two of smokes.

I needed to get away from Red. Away from his crew. In a world where shivs were in most pockets, where guys shot up dope and worked out all day, and where correction officers would walk slow to a conflict in hopes a fight would end before they got to it, it was a tough ask. In fact, I didn't know anyone inside Pine Mountain to ask. I needed help and I needed someone who had more to offer than a tattoo gun or TV antenna.

It was Sunday and I went that day for the first time to the chapel. There I prayed to the big man upstairs. I was never a big believer till that day in God or angels or anything involving the dead. But I am now. I know beyond a doubt the big man is real and so are spirits. I ain't bragging that I know, just telling the truth. I asked if God would send some help. He did. Noah ark style. It started raining that afternoon and it rained all night. Pine Mountain is the only prison I know of in the US that only has two outside walls. Even places like Alcatraz on an island has walls on four sides. Not Pine. The sides are hemmed in by two mountain cliffs. Truth be told, the back wall is mostly show and not really necessary either. It is nothing but mountain cliff there as well. Those mountains can't be climbed. Nothing can go up. But that ain't stopping things from coming down. And when it rains, the water off those three mountain sides comes down into the bowl where Pine sits like the floodwaters of the Bible. It was often that the storm drains overflowed. Less often it was ankle deep in A Block. I had seen A Block flood once in my short term. But never the whole prison. On this night Pine risked being underwater even in the high spots.

I got called by Dora to the grate by the whipping post. Somehow the grate popped open and something flowed down into the hole. Now it was blocking the flow through the tunnel and into the mines. The water had nowhere to go but up. If something weren't done soon, the backup would flood the yard and the officer's quarters. While some prisoners lay sandbags and stood scooping water into barrels as it came over, me and another guy were told to swim down and unclog the tunnel so the water had somewhere to go.

Seemed like a suicide mission to be sure, but I was a good swimmer. Ain't bragging. It is just the way it is. My partner couldn't get down without panicking. I could. I dove down and found a wheelbarrow jammed crooked in the hole. Other trash piled around it. I poked at the trash like you might poke rice down the holes in your kitchen sink. Two trips later, I got that wheelbarrow turned and it swooped down the tunnel. So did all the water backed up. So did I.

I emptied out in a wide space in the tunnels I was dying and just grabbing for anything. I caught some loose rebar and climbed my way out of the water flow onto a bank. A few feet from me there was a metal grate someone put in to prevent escape. The wheelbarrow was against it, but it was big enough that it wouldn't matter. As I found a dry patch above me I put my hand on something. I ain't making this up, there was a skeleton. You ain't been scared till you are trapped underground with bones.

I wanted to run, but nowhere to go. Dark too. So, I made peace with him. Moved a little closer and then closer still till I could touch him. Strangest thing, he had an eye – I kid you not, a glass eye. Sitting right there like brand new in his skull. I can't tell you why, but I pocketed that eye. Maybe just to look at later in the light. But truth told I wanted it. Then I shuffled up a little higher, just so wouldn't be sitting on the bones. There I found a small box. Curiosity got me and I opened it. Dynamite. Up high in that tunnel it was still dry to. I know me some dynamite.

I waited down there all night safe and sound. No Big Red. In the morning I was able to walk through the water up the tunnel and back to the pit below the grate. Officers helped me out and made it clear I did a good job keeping them dry. I was valuable. I met their need and in Pine that means something even between a guard and a prisoner.

Red hadn't forgotten about me though. He nicknamed me "Li'l Pig" or "McPig." He thought that last one was hysterical. Told everyone "Mc" in his culture meant "son of." Of course, everyone laughed. That was the correct response when Red told a joke, even a bad one. I wondered if he just kept me alive just to tell his joke. He wasn't smart enough to come up with something every day and "McPig" bought me some time as it was better to get a laugh than rid the world of a dumb criminal whose dad just happened to be a cop.

Every need a debt. I found my currency amongst other prisoners in the slop house. I got assigned to pick up the trash and clean the slop in the kitchen. Red thought that was an even better twist on being McPig, now wallowing in everyone else's slop. So, I survived being the trash boy. More importantly, I found they ran a hose with hot water every night to ensure no pipes froze. Convinced an inmate over in cooking to go in with me. We wrapped that hose around a metal trash can with my ingredients. Yellow corn starch, sugar, yeast, a little ketchup and a few other items cooked low and slow with that hot water coil. Took a week, but we made our first batch of Julep wine.

My fortunes changed when I became the lead shiner on premises. Big Red still called me McPig but the harshness wasn't in the jab anymore. Especially since I made sure he got his julep for free. Every need a debt. One year in and I thought I was through the worst. I kept the glass eye with my personal stuff in my cell as a reminder of my good turn of fortune.

Got my cell moved in the spring. Came to find out my bunk had been for a short while James Earl's bed. The man who killed MLK Jr. Not much to that. Rumor was it was James Earl haunted the cell, but he wasn't the disturbed presence I would encounter. Cell was wide enough to stand up, not much more. One corner had a toilet. The other a sink and single outlet. I still had my coffee maker set up under the outlet. Two beds, one over another. I always chose the top. Just felt safer. Stay aloft. Stay unseen unless someone wanted to crack a joke about me. I hit the balance between a non-threat, the butt of a joke, and an essential part of yard life. Ain't bragging, just saying how it was. I made my Julep, ate my cheeseburger every ten days or so, got active in the chapel, saw my dad when he came to visit, and did my time.

Only channel I got was ABC. Channel 10. Got me Three's Company, Happy Days, an occasional football game, Ripley's Believe It Or Not, and the news. It is a most peculiar thing, watching the news. You are surrounded by hardened criminals. You see violence daily. But watching someone bigger than life on the news like Hanson Robertson was captivating. For several months on the news they showed the same image of him sneering at the camera before entering court. A murderer for hire, his last kill he did for $1500. Didn't know the guy or anything. Just took the money and executed the man the next day. Apparently had eleven or so kills previously. This one just happened to be a judge and he got caught. Good enough state lawyer kept him out of Ole Sparky. Pled guilty and sentenced to life in Pine Mountain. He spent the two days in solitaire before assigned to the cell next to me on A Block. Oh, the news also reported that the cop who arrested him was my dad.

Hanson was not suited to be a head down, low key prisoner. First week he came and sat next to my cellmate at dinner. Table was so narrow my tray touched Hanson's across the table. I could smell his sweat and BO. His greasy, unwashed hair hung low into his own food and as he talked, strands of it swung up and over my own tray. My stomach lurched.

I was lucky being across from him. My roommate was right next to him, elbow to elbow. Hanson pulled a fork filed down on the handle end to make a shiv and stuck it into my roommate's armpit. He started to squeal but Hanson put a hand over his mouth.

"Keep it quiet. You scream or motion for help. Even let them know you're cut while I'm here, you die. I hear you have dope. Give it to me." Hanson twisted the knife. My cellmate kicked my shins under the table as a response. I almost let out a cry but the rancid smell of Hanson's breath worked like smelling salts, bringing me to attention. Quiet, stock still attention.

"I-" my roomie started to say something and then gasped. A small moan left his mouth and his eyes rolled backwards as the shiv went a little deeper. My cellmate used his good arm to reach in a pocket and pull out a match box. Inside was a hit, maybe two, of dope. Hanson took it and removed the shiv. I kept my head down, eating my meatloaf as Hanson scooted back and left the table with his tray for another seat in the hall. My cellmate took his napkin and placed it under his arm. Blood ran down his sleeve. He clamped the napkin between his arm and side, crying. He cried all the way back to the cell where he finally told a guard he was bleeding. They asked him who did it. He refused to tell. Guards gave me a day in solitary to see if I would talk. Neither of us gave up Hanson's name. My cellmate's wound got infected. A few days later he was dead. Lost his life for two hits of dope. I'm just telling you so you know. That's life in Pine.

Story went that Hanson's old man, also a Hanson but went by "Handsome Robertson" escaped Pine Mountain. He and another guy snuck out at night. The other one was found the next day in the drainage tunnel with his head bashed in by a rock. Handsome Robertson was never found. Most assumed he died somewhere lost in the mines. Hanson Jr, aka Bigs, said his dad made it out and even came to see him every year on his birthday. Might even have the balls to come visit Hanson in prison. No one argued. Hanson was too tall, too wide, and too filled with a cool rage to argue with. That left a problem for Big Red.

Hanson soon became known as "Bigs." And there weren't going to be two "Bigs" in the yard. I was working the slop house, separating the trash out under the porch to the cafeteria. Had a good view of the yard. Big Red was lifting weights. Looked like had three or four of the forty-five pounders on each side. Did two reps and then groaned with the third. His two buddies started to spot him. One took a shiv to the side by Bigs. The other spotter stood between Hanson and Big Red, abandoning his spotting duties for the sake of bodyguard ones.

The weight bar swayed before falling on Big Red's chest. I can't be certain, but I bet the pop I heard was his ribs breaking like matchsticks struck too hard. The other spotter took a step toward Bigs before two of Bigs recruits lifted him from his feet. Several smaller fights started around the yard as Hanson's crew, mostly guys on the outs with Red, took to Red's crew.

The CO near me starting the slowest walk I'd ever seen. I know I watched for a full thirty seconds before he even walked ten paces. My great grandma could walk faster and she's in her late nineties. I looked around. None of the other officers were moving any quicker. They were going to let this one play out before they got involved. That's the way it was in Pine Mountain.

Hanson "Bigs" Robertson simply rolled that bar back off Red's chest and onto his windpipe. Crushed, Red's face contorted as if his final breath of life was focused on looking intently at his knees down at the other end of the bench. Hanson stepped away and walked casually back to a nearby bench. The guards blew whistles for us to return to our cells. Red's body sat there for nearly a day as did three others whose blood ran in the storm grates. We all stayed in lockup till the coroner arrived the next afternoon.

The next day I got my new cellmate. Basil. Basil Quenton Ott. I hadn't seen him in the yard, though several times in the chapel. Figured he must be from B Block. His clothes were tattered and grungy rather than the new ones given to a fresh fish, so I didn't ask anything more than if he was okay with the bottom bunk. That night I was watching Three's Company and he stood over my shoulder. He didn't have a TV so I felt obligated to share. I slid over and asked if he could see.

"Is it... Are those people..."

"Three's Company," I offered.

"Three's Company," he repeated. Then, "I never seen anything like it."

"I know," I said as Suzanne Somers stepped into the living room for her scene. "She's a wonder."

I went to bed after, but Basil stayed up till the station put up that rainbow screen notifying all program was closed for the day. Back then, TV wasn't 24-7 like it is now, you know. Some of you remember.

Next morning our door opened and I stepped out for line to breakfast. Halfway down the hall I looked back to tell Basil I thought it was sausage link day. He wasn't there. I glimpsed back further, risking a warning from Dora. He was nowhere in line. That was when I had my first suspicion Basil wasn't really in prison at Pine Mountain. Well, at least not in the same way I was.

I saw him in chapel and went to sit by him. "Where you go, man? This morning?"

He said nothing.

"I mean, when we went to breakfast. You weren't in line and weren't in the cell neither."

His head was nearly bald except for three long strands that matted up. They were like ropes left in the water too long and covered in green slime. Two swooped over his bald head and one rebelled, falling be-tween his two eyes. Those eyes narrowed and a flash of orange shown behind his blue eyes. "That thing last night, 'Three's Company,' will it be on again tonight?"

I didn't know exactly what to do with the shift in conversation, but decided it best to talk about what he wanted to discuss. "No, not tonight. Likely Laverne and Shirley."

"Laverne and Shirley." It was more statement than question.

"Yeah, But seriously. Why were you not-"

The chaplain stopped his reading of Psalm 23 to stare in our direc-tion. "Kolby, who are you talking to? The spirit got your tongue?"

I looked next to me to signal I was just talking to my roommate. There was no one there.

During my yard time I ventured from my normal post under the deck of the cafeteria that served as the slop house and my Julep opera-tion. I walked the perimeter of the fence line so far as we were allowed till I came to the small cemetery of inmates in the back corner. There I paused. I'd say I was stirred by the almighty. You know, sometimes he don't speak direct. Sometimes it is just that gentle nudge or change in the wind. Or maybe it was just fool's luck. I walked around the old tombstones, kicking a fallen pine cone as I went. It was the second row deep I saw it. Basil Quenton Ott. D Oct 14, 1967. The name was sketched with same kindergarten luster mine and most prison tattoos held. But there was no denying what it said. My new roommate died in 1967.

That night my cell was empty. Basil never came back to sleep nor to watch Laverne and Shirley. I was freaking out. There is probably a more eloquent way to say that and if I ever paid attention in school, I would say it that way. But all I know is it was the second time in Pine

Mountain I cried myself to sleep. I knew I had to be losing my mind. Only explanation.

Maybe the fact I didn't sleep is why I was slow when doors opened the next morning. As I stepped out into the hallway into a line already a bit in motion, I felt a shove and pushed back into my cell. My back hit the wall, still sweating with last night's humidity. Bigs reached down and lifted me up. His foul breath swept across me like a tornado to a trailer park. He said but one thing before setting me back to the ground. "McPig. Your dad ain't just a cop. He is the cop. The one put me in here."

Jenson, the CO that morning, tapped Bigs on the back with his baton. "Let's get moving."

Bigs raised his hands up in an "I comply" gesture before leaving my cell. I stood and moved to the door. Blocking my way was Basil. I swear I didn't see him in the cell with me. The place ain't that big.Wherever he had been, he was there now with a hand on either side of the opening. He turned his head back toward me. "That was Robertson. Wasn't it."

"Where have you been? Who are-"

"Wasn't it?" Basil's eyes flashed that orange again. His lip curled in to a snarl and I swear I saw not one, but two rows of teeth accentuating his rage.

"Yeah. I mean, his name is Robertson. Hanson Robertson. Everyone calls him Bigs."

Jenson's voice prevailed. "No one gives a rat's ass what someone's name is in here McPig. Get in line."

With that, Basil again disappeared. He wasn't in chapel either, but I thought he wouldn't miss Three's Company. I was right. I ain't bragging. Nothing to brag about over the next few days of this story.

That night Basil reappeared. This time I saw it. His bunk was empty and then it wasn't. No flash of light or nothing. Just there. I started to ask him a question and he hushed me. So, we watched the Fonz wear wooden water skis and jump over a shark. I kid you not. There I was watching Henry Winkler jump over a killer shark while the man who wanted to kill me was one cell over and I shared my room with a dead man.

When it was over, I turned off the TV. Basil protested, his eyes saddened almost like a young boy not getting his ice cream. But I had to know. "You died. I saw your gravestone."

He paused, moving that rebel strand of hair back into the poor excuse for a combover.

Then I added. "That's why you love the TV. Didn't have those when you was in here, I bet?"

"No," Basil said softly. I got the feeling he was sorting this out every bit as much as me. "No, I suppose we didn't. When I came in to Pine Mountain houses didn't have TV's. No way a prisoner got one. We worked the mines. Slept, ate, and worked the mines." His eyes drifted back to the TV. "I wouldn't mind watching a little more."

I took a chance. "First, I'd like to know why you got so mad at Robertson."

His eyes narrowed again and that flash of orange reappeared. I can't confirm but I think the room went darker. I know at least the light flickered. "Robertson. He's the one who put me in the grave."

"Couldn't be him. I mean, his dad maybe. You died before Bigs probably even out of elementary school. His dad go by the name Handsome Robertson."

The flash in Basil's eyes and the sneer, showing that second row of teeth. This time I know there were two rows. One his own and one from somewhere inside him, like a demon using Basil's restless spirit as his own conduit. "Yes." The response came out as a hiss.

"Well, he's after me," I said. Figured might as well put all my cards on the table, honest like. I was always an honest guy. Ain't bragging, just saying how it is. "My dad is a cop. Not just a cop, he's the cop who arrested Bigs, Hanson Jr. I mean. Says I'm next on his kill list."

"No. Bring him to me. I wants him." Basil ground his teeth and his sunken jaw popped like it came unhinged. His restless hair dropped in front of his face. "Blood for blood. Blood for blood."

"He's next door. Why don't you just go get him?"

"Can't. No power here. Can't."

"Then how do I see you?"

Basil pointed to the bed. I followed his finger and then remembered. "That eye. That was your eye, wasn't it?" When I turned back, he was gone.

Another two days went by and no sign of Basil. I spent my time avoiding Bigs. I had one close encounter in the cafeteria. He sat down right next to me and I remembered that shiv he had. I dumped my tray all in my lap and fell backwards. Lost my chance at meatloaf, one of my faves, and spent the day in solitary but survived the day.

The next day in the yard I knew I would have no such luck. One of Bigs underlings came over to Jenson, the guard who normally stood outside the slop pit so he could smoke in the shade. He handed Jenson something – money, dope, or maybe both, and Jenson got up and left. The goon looked over at Bigs and then nodded his head. Bigs dropped his dumbbells onto the concrete and started toward me.

I was cornered under the deck of the cafeteria. My hot water Julep production on one side, garbage bins on the other and the cafeteria building behind me. The door in was not an option, locked except at night when I did trash.

Bigs stood in the only exit. Two more of his goons joined the third who paid off Jenson. "McPig. McPiggy Wiggy. McScrewed is what I say. Let's see what daddy says when he finds out I put his little baby McPiggy six feet under."

I reached up and grabbed the hot steam pipe my copper ran around. I jerked it with all my weight and the pipe came loose. A gush of hot water poured out just as Bigs moved in close. My hand was burnt, probably down to the muscle. But so was Bigs' shoulder and arm. He screamed and I ran.

Startled, the three behind Big didn't grab me. If they had, no one would be telling this tale. Ain't bragging, but I can be a fast little booger when I need to be. But fast don't help much in a small yard. And Bigs had lots of guys willing to see my life end if it meant doing Bigs a favor. Every need a debt. Cornering me created a good debt for anyone fearful of Bigs. And everyone in the yard was scared of Bigs. I hadn't seen anyone, not even the guards, stand up to him.

Except. The last few days I had carried that glass eye with me. I felt it against my hip and put my finger in my pocket. They touched the smooth marble like texture. There was one who saw Bigs without flinching in fear. One who instead of cowering, snarled. Snarled with that extra set of teeth and flash of orange in his eyes.

"Bring him to me," I remembered as Basil's last words. I scanned the yard, desperate to see Basil running toward my station, ready to help. He was nowhere. Just a group of guys forming a circle around me as Bigs made his way closer.

Then I saw the whipping post. The grate underneath is how Bigs' dad and Basil escaped. It was the tunnel out. Or at least it was for Handsome Robertson. Handsome bashed Basil's head in rather than share the taste of freedom. Who knows the why, but he left something to rot in that tunnel. Not the body, that was found and buried. He left Basil Quenton Ott's soul down there. And it hungered. It was ravenous. It sat. No, it lulled about that drain.

I ran. It was a life-or-death game of Red Rover as I burst through two men trying to keep me in the circle. They couldn't hold me. A few paces and I stopped at the whipping post. I scanned around. No guard was moving as Bigs closed in.

"Ain't nowhere for McPiggy to go. You are mine now, copper's boy."

He stepped closer. One foot onto the grate. Then another. His breath smelled of old cigarettes and hard-boiled eggs just past their goodness. He reared back his arm to throw a punch and I held out the glass eye.

"Basil. See. See him? Handsome's boy. Let us down there, you hear?"

Everyone watching must've thought I'd gone mad. That is until the grate beside me shot up and landed a good twenty feet away in the yard. I didn't hesitate. I jumped down in that pit. Bigs followed. I heard his leg crunch as he landed. His scream echoed all around me. Disorienting if I hadn't been here before.

I entered that tunnel. It was bone dry today. I heard behind me, "I'm comin McPiggy. This is where you die."

I got to that ledge and climbed. Bigs was moving slower, but he would be along any minute. As he came through the tunnel he scanned for me in the dim light. He saw that wheelbarrow, still there and now turned over.

"Hiding under there like a little piggy? Time to make you squeal." He moved to the wheelbarrow and lifted it ready to pummel the man he thought hiding underneath. Problem was, I wasn't there.

I was on the ledge with a stick of dynamite. I ran my fingers up it to check if it was good. In the dark no way of knowing for sure, but time didn't allow any luxuries. I lit my Zippo. Then the wick sparked to life. I tossed it down the ledge between the exit and Bigs.

There was a "What the hell!" as Bigs realized something near him had a fuse. He may have even tried to outrun it, but I don't think so. Not hurt like he was. The explosion collapsed the tunnel. Fortunately, I was fast enough to get clear and back to the pit below the grate.

The next week a crew dug out the tunnel so the next rain would have a place to go. When they came to Bigs the story goes he wasn't crushed by rock. The area he was in stayed open. He was dead though. Folk down there clearing say it was most horrible thing they ever saw. He had peeled his own skin loose scratching and tugging. All his fingers were broken and snapped. I know that wasn't the case when he was chasing me. And his face. His face they say was nothing but terror. Folk knew I had yelled for Basil. It didn't take long to put it together. And they knew Basil made sure Bigs' final moments on this earth were a foretaste of the hell he had waiting.

I finished my time in peace. Kept that eye in my pocket. No one took it from me either. Figure they were too scared. I was no longer McPig. I was Kolby. New bullies in the yard were quickly told the story and even quicker gave me a wide berth. The next few years I made my Julep, did my time, and watched the new comedies on ABC. On occasion Basil would join and watch with me. I guess you could say we were friends of a sort. I ain't bragging that I'm friends with a ghost or that he and I took down Hanson Brigs Robertson, son of Handsome Robertson. I ain't bragging at all. Ain't nothing to brag about in Pine Mountain. But it happened. And I'm just telling you so you know the truth of it.

Happy Mother's Day

J ust because I carry it well, doesn't mean it isn't heavy.

I saw my mother today. By chance. Not by intent.

I was in the store with my youngest daughter in the grocery cart. She was playing with a can of cream style corn and a box of instant rice. I think it was her Wal-Mart Barbie and Ken.

My mother asked my daughter's name, and I told her. I gave her the formal "Lorena" rather than "Lori." There was power in that decision that I needed to convey, even if my mother didn't know I had made such a choice.

My mother moved her coat surreptitiously over her single grocery item, Miller High Life. I remember her joke. Every parent has that joke they say too often and think it is funnier than it is. "In dog beers, I've only had one!" She would laugh and laugh.

Her cart blocked my path. In my youth, I had to either turn and run or charge. Children don't get to choose their trauma. They can hide from it in a closet or tell it that it can't hurt them. But the scars prove otherwise.

Today I am not that trapped child. And my daughter, though in the cage of a shopping cart, will be freer than I ever was. A new me speaks.

"I got my five-year chip last week," I announced. I did not move the cart as I took the chip out of my pocket. My eyes instructed my mother not to come any closer, like that five-year chip was garlic or holy water to a vampire. I placed the chip back in my pocket, but now we both knew it could be brought out again.

I have survived much. One resident baby-daddy made me eat on the floor from a dog bowl when my mother announced her pregnancy with his child. My mother laughed and drank. In dog beers, she had maybe three that night.

Once my mother screamed and threw things. Her boyfriends played rough first with her then with me. That was the first time I took the white pills. My mother gave them to me.

I escaped by running away. But the rabbit hole I chased led me to many a mad hatter and Cheshire cats. Indeed, if I was Alice, then my mother was the Queen of Hearts.

But I am not Alice. Not all girls are made of sugar and spice and everything nice. Some are made of alcohol, sarcasm, and meanness. I am made of the same bolt of cloth as my mother.

I have felt her sorrows as I relived them in my own life. Unemployment. Abuse. Miscarriages. Broken Relationships. Homelessness. Sure, I chose whiskey and heroin over beer and pills. Window dressings but I lived in the same cottage.

I remember the day I realized I had run away from my mom to become just like her.

And at that moment as my mind traverses the darker underbrush of my adolescence, I almost speak to my mother. I almost invited her over to see her granddaughter. I practically embrace not only her but all the memories of her trying to be a mom. The time she bought me a strawberry shortcake doll or let me decorate my brother's birthday cake.

A tenderness stirs inside me. Not all in her suffering was her doing. She too had a mother. She too had bruises and scars from a life she did not ask to live. I almost speak again. I almost tell Lori, "This is your grandmother."

Just because I carry it well, doesn't mean it isn't heavy.

I think my mother knew I was breaking. She takes a step toward my grocery cart. Can-corn Barbie and Rice-Box Ken were, after all, having an engagement party.

She does not know Lori, Lorena to her. She only knows my teen son. I see him tonight on visitation. His father's parents, who have custody, have allowed me that treasure. I know they worry more about his meal with me each week than they do him being out late on a Friday night with friends. They are right to worry. But they have seen my work. They know I have done what their son couldn't do.

I feel the five-year chip's comforting weight in my pocket. I recover my resolve.

I have fought. I have stopped listening to who I can't be, and allowed myself to be who I am.

My eyes remember. I do not recall the hardest part of my childhood. That would be like picking one grain of sand as your favorite part of the beach. I remembered that I learned to hold on until tomorrow — a combination of sheer stubbornness and self-love.

I always wear pants with pockets these days, and my fingers slip in my pocket and touch the sobriety chip. I felt the chip enter my bloodstream and speak to my soul.

The temptation passes, and I again see my mom's coat over her Miller High Life, the champagne of beers. In my mind, I picture my mom in her bedraggled state at a fine dinner party making a toast. I almost laugh at the image.

My mother never fit her skin. It was not just the physical brutality of drugs. Her soul wanted to shed her body and be somewhere else. Anywhere else. Any "Who-else." But she never had the strength to change.

As a teenager, she would disappear. Sometimes literally disappear, and I would play mother to my half-siblings. Sometimes her physical presence would be there sprawled out on a couch amongst her own wreckage and the debris. Those were the hardest times.

No, not everyone has a loving mother. But I love my mother. I know now I can love her without allowing in her toxicity. I can love without feeling bullied, without feeling worthless, without feeling responsible for her decisions.

For me, to learn to love meant leaving my sisters and brother. Those chains almost held me in the imprisonment of what is my family. I passionately loved them. I defended them. I attacked others who would dare devalue them. But the irony is I loved them and still didn't know what love was. I managed the trauma so we could live another day. And I defended my mother even when I knew there was no defense.

After all, if my mother was not a good woman, how was I to be of any value myself?

When I finally ran, I kept score of my value. Money never gave me value nor did relationships. Drugs didn't provide value, but they gave relief from its pursuit, at least temporarily. But they also taught me that I was unlovable.

I am not unlovable — a double negative. I am lovable. And being lovable may be the hardest thing for an addict to carry. It is a weighty truth.

My mind drew me back to the present standoff. My mother continued to stand, blocking the aisle. Corn-Barbie and Rice-Box Ken were now driving somewhere in a Capri-sun box. I think it was a Kiwi – Strawberry Ferrari. Or maybe a minivan.

"She is so pretty," my mother spoke. "She has my... your eyes."

Today I set out to:

- Clean my apartment
- Go by the thrift store, Lori needs some new shoes
- Give myself a pedicure
- Buy groceries for the week
- Make dinner and serve with cupcakes for Lori and my teenage son
- Read Lori a story before bedtime
- Not drink or use

There is flexibility. I want to get a nicer pair of shoes for Lori so I might wait till next payday. The grocery list didn't include a snackable, but it is her favorite. So, I will likely get her two or seven. I may or may not make the cupcakes.

There is also rigidity in my list. I will not drink or use. I will not place myself in an environment where such opportunities are readily available. My life will not venture into entropy.

I raised my arm to stop my mother's approach. As I did, the track marks on my wrist became exposed. Five years since the last, but the scars remain.

I don't trust anyone without scars. I don't trust people who aren't willing to be scarred for their commitments whether it be giving birth, jumping a ramp on a bicycle, or eating tacos.

My outward scars show many of my bad decisions. But they also show the birth of my daughter by C-Section, the weight I've added now that I am clean, and the general bruises and cuts from working an honest job in a factory.

My inward scars are much uglier. Some are callused, and some are still bleeding.

My mother would tell me my arms are ugly. Tell me I'm not beautiful, I'm not of value, I'm not enough.

I used to yell back that I was or tell her why she could never be loved either.

Or sometimes I would just run. Run and hide. Run, and self-loathe. Run, and self-hurt.

But today I just stand in the aisle surrounded by paper plates and bathroom cleaners. On my left are all things disposable and on my right the chemicals to remove the memory of an accident. I am neither. So here I stand. I can do no other.

This is the mom Lori will have. A mom with scars and a five-year chip. A mom who loves herself enough to get up the next day and live.

I am not that little girl I once was. I love my mother. But unconditional love means that you love even when you may not be loved back. She takes another step toward my outstretched hand. She wobbles a bit and is unsteady in her gate. Her breath is now close enough to be recognizable. The alcohol, the cigarettes, the years of poor hygiene, poor choices, and ruined aspirations.

Perhaps the woman I've always loved is still there and is fighting for control. Control to make a decision.

Corn-Barbie and Rice-Box Ken finish their adventure in their Capri-Sun minivan. I see now it is definitely a minivan, as Lori's hopes are tied up in being like her mother. I am proud of my minivan. And I'm proud of the work I did to purchase it.

I nudge my cart forward. My mother moves her cart to the side.

It is perhaps the kindest thing she has ever done. I am now free to go forward on my own terms. There are Snackables ahead and hopefully time to make cupcakes. I like the yellow ones with cream cheese icing. Lori loves sprinkles on them.

I move into the next aisle where the cereal is, and I feel a tear roll down my eye. Now that it is safe I hear myself whisper on this Sunday afternoon,

Special Preview: Hold On Tight

THE FIRST CHAPTER FROM JERRY HARWOOD'S NEW BOOK HOLD ON TIGHT

P lease enjoy the first few pages. Hold On Tight by Jerry Harwood is available at Amazon.com. Visit Jerry Harwood's website:

CHAPTER ONE:

As Megan slammed the driver-side door, she realized only too late the end of her long, flowing scarf remained inside. She felt her shoulders and neck revolt against the rest of her body. The color-coded, highlighted, and well-organized wedding binder did not have the same attachment to the car door as her scarf. It went forward, scattering over the parking lot. The wedding schedule, names of family members and important friends, the order for the toasts, and the marriage certificate took flight.

Megan reached out in an attempt to pull the folder and the last ten seconds of her life back in. As she did, gravity won out. She hit her back against the car door and slumped to the ground. Frantically, she unwrapped the knitted noose from her neck. As she stood, the wind caught the loose papers. At first, they were aflutter near her feet. Then the wind, perhaps realizing how it might continue to torment her, sent a stronger gust.

Megan eyed the envelope with the marriage certificate. It was tenuously holding its flight pattern over a puddle. She lurched forward, far from gracefully, toward the envelope. Her fingers touched the edge before the wind chose to take it a bit farther down the pea gravel parking lot. The marriage certificate danced over the neighboring spaces before landing against the sidewalk's curb. From there, it caught an upward draft straight into the holly bushes with the reception song list.

Megan removed the scarf and moved toward the holly bush. She heard the snap of her left shoe's heel. Her reward was a skinned knee and another trip to the gravel lot. Her new circular-frame eyeglasses decided they would abandon ship and bounced a few feet away. Megan sat on her bottom, feeling the ground's moisture creep up her skirt. She raised her hands before patting the ground around her. A deluge of tears threatened to explode from her eyes as she strained to keep them at bay.

Frank closed the passenger side door and stretched. He was chuckling. He walked around the car, and picked the keys off the ground. He clicked the remote and the car gave its resonant "beep, beep." Frank reached to check that the door was locked before bending over to offer Megan help up.

Megan took his hand and lifted herself off the ground. Her knee had a small trickle of blood and some gravel clinging to the wound.

Frank unlocked the driver-side door, releasing the captive scarf. He scooped the scarf off the ground as he said, "Right in a puddle. You probably ruined it. And I just bought this for you too."

"I'm sorry," Megan said. She continued to brush off the gravel dust from her blouse and seasonal skirt. Her skirt had a damp section. Her hair pin had been shifted so her curly mop of hair threatened to burst loose from its cage. She figured it probably looked like a hornet's nest, if it was indeed even that orderly. She looked back at Frank. "Will you help me." she pleaded.

"That holly bush will rip these suede pants to smithereens. But I tell you what, sweetie, I'll go see if I can find someone to come help you." With that, Frank walked off toward the barn. Megan had no time to waste. She walked over to the holly bush. Bending over, she felt a jolt of pain in her bad knee. She scolded the bush with a pointed finger as she reached in for her envelope. Reclaiming the marriage certificate cost her a thorn and a new tear in her blouse. She avoided having anything prickly barb her legs, though. Megan thanked her mother for her genes. Being 6'2" had its advantages when arguing with holly bushes.

Megan collected her other papers, assembling them in as much an order as she could muster. The once-pristine notebook now looked like something out of a third grader's bookbag. Limping back to the car, she pulled the door latch. She had a repair kit for her heels. *A wedding planner must be ready for anything!* The Prius was locked. She scanned the parking lot for Frank. There were several people talking nearby, but he was not among them. She felt the perspiration on her brow. A man in a tux pointed at his watch. He tapped it before looking around the parking lot. *Looking for me. He is looking for his wedding planner.*

Her own watch said 3:45. She wanted to be early, and, officially, she had fifteen minutes before she was late. Megan took off her good shoe. She snapped the heel off and returned it to her foot. *Better to have two things broken the same way, than hobble along with one good and one bad.* She picked up the now empty folder. Slowly, she began walking to each scattered paper, placing a foot on it to stop its movement, and reclaiming it to the folder. Then, materials in hand, she stumbled down the sidewalk toward the front door of the barn and the wedding party.

*****

The large double barn doors had tea lights strung around the outside eave of the door. There was an antique, oak table with a sign-in book displayed and a washtub below, tied with a strip of burlap. A few gifts sat in the tub along with some cards. Behind the table were several men in tuxes.

"Excuse me," Megan said. "Are one of you the groom?"

"That's me," said a man in his early twenties. He had a trimmed beard and his hair pulled back in a manbun. He looked up to Megan, who was a head taller. His breath smelled of the bourbon he had likely consumed to calm his nerves.

"I'm Megan Rouche. I am the wedding planner. Well, actually, I am her assistant."

"I thought my fiancée hired a woman named ..." The groom looked up in the sky as if to see if the name was written there.

"Caroline. Caroline Tipton," Megan offered.

"Yes. I met her. She was, um, shorter and..." the groom trailed off.

Megan realized his comments may have been more bourbon than actual opinion. This was his wedding, and until now he had no wedding planner on site. And now, he had one he had never met who probably looked like she just arrived from a ten-day backpacking trip in the wild. As if to punctuate the point, her hair clip chose that moment to spring away from her head. It fell to the floor as her curly, long hair cascaded down. She pulled her hair out of her face and gave her best smile. "Yes, and she was your wedding planner. Is, I mean. She is pregnant. Or was pregnant. She is in delivery right now."

Megan watched the groom and his groomsmen process the information. "What is important is that she sent me to help. I am sorry, I had a fall in the parking lot. Could one of you point me to the bathroom? And then help me find the bride?"

One of the groomsmen stepped forward. "I'll take you. I heard Sarah is freaking out."

"Thanks," Megan said. And then with a groan to herself more than the groomsman, "We got this."

As she followed the groomsman into the barn, Frank walked around the corner with an elderly man beside him. "Megan! There you are. I found someone to get those papers out of the bush for you."

"Not now Frank," was Megan's reply. She continued walking as Frank lifted his arms in a "why did I even bother" gesture.

*****

Sarah was pacing the hallway outside the dressing room in her bridal dress. A man in khakis and a flannel shirt sat nearby her. He held a Bible in his hand and had a folding chair leaned back on two legs. His head was resting against the wall with his eyes closed. Kinley passed by him, dropping a used tissue carelessly on the floor.

A bridesmaid was attempting to keep pace with Kinley. She was holding a box of tissues, handing Sarah new ones as she collected the used.

Megan approached the two women. She checked her hairclip and ran her hand on her neck. She wished she had her scarf as she always felt her neck was too long for her body. But her short jaunt in the bathroom only allowed time to tuck in her blouse, wipe her knee, and reposition her hair. She swallowed before speaking. "Kinley? I'm Megan. Caroline sent me."

Kinley stopped a few feet from Megan. Teary-eyed she said, "Where is Caroline?"

"She is so very sorry. She went into delivery this morning."

Kinley began weeping again. She grew louder and another bridesmaid poked her head out of the dressing area. The man in the flannel shirt set his chair down on all fours and waved her to come join Sarah, Megan, and the other bridesmaids. The second bridesmaid joined the group of ladies. She, too, had a box of tissues at the ready. Sarah grabbed one from each bridesmaid as she continued crying.

Megan took a tissue from the bridesmaid box. Then she tilted Kinley's chin upward and began wiping the mascara smudges away with the tissue. "Listen. Kinley. We got this. Okay."

Kinley's sob lessened but did not cease. Megan looked at the two bridesmaids. "What are your names, dear?"

The girl looked up from the tissue box. "Nancy." The other added, "Lila."

"Nancy and Lila, you take Kinley back to the dressing room. Touch up her makeup. Then play a favorite song. If that doesn't help, then you all do some karaoke. I'm serious. Makeup, then music. Understand."

Nancy and Lila nodded. Then Megan looked back to Kinley. "I will tell the audience to be patient. We will begin ten minutes late, but there are NO PROBLEMS. You understand? None. We got this. Your fiancé is here. He loves you. You are here. You love him. Everything will work out. I will make sure of it, okay."

Kinley hugged Megan as she whispered, "Thank you. But, what about the pastor?"

Megan took Kinley by the shoulders and looked into her tear-stained eyes. "I will take care of it."

Nancy and Lila led Kinley through the door to the ladies' dressing area. Megan took a moment to look in the hallway mirror. There were still a few uncooperative strands of curls. She removed the hair clip, used her fingers as a comb, and attempted to wrangle in all of her hair before reattaching the clip. One rebellious strand escaped and hung down by her cheek. She sighed. Then, remembering her own pep talk to Kinley, she smiled into the mirror.

When she turned from the mirror, she saw the man in the flannel shirt was watching her. Her eyes followed the length of his broad shoulders and down his muscular arms to the Bible he was holding. She cleared her throat. "And you, you need to go get dressed into something more appropriate. I need you in front of everyone in ten minutes."

"Ma'am, I don't think-"

Megan cut him off. She pointed at the Bible. "You are a pastor? Right?"

"Well, yes. I mean I am, but-"

"Then get going. You have a job to do. Ten minutes and I want you up front and ready. Have the groom with you." Megan paused before adding, "And get him some mouthwash. Kinley doesn't want to kiss bourbon lips."

"Are you always this demanding and decisive?" the man asked, chuckling.

Megan ignored the comment. "I'll start sending in the groomsmen and bridesmaids in pairs in twenty minutes. Right now, I need to go tell everyone waiting we are on a short delay."

The man's smile widened. "Perhaps you should let me do that." His eyes directed her to the tear in her blouse and then to her long, but skinned-up legs.

Megan knew he was right. She was not the best face to go before a gathering to offer calm and reassurance that everything was okay. Still, she thought, this man was exceedingly rude. She began to tell him so, but he had already walked away. "Okay, you do it," she said trying make it her decision. He turned and moved toward the front of the barn where the groom and groomsmen were.

On her way, Megan kept an eye out for Frank. If she saw him, she would have him go to the car and get her scarf and maybe even dig her running shoes out of his backseat if they were there. But Frank was nowhere in sight.

The groomsmen were no longer loitering outside. She went to the nearby guys' dressing area and knocked to let them know she was there. As she did, she saw the tattoo on her wrist that said in a simple cursive, "Hold on tight." She thought, *I didn't quite mean it like this, but I suppose it still applies.*

www.ingramcontent.com/pod-product-compliance
Lightning Source LLC
Chambersburg PA
CBHW070412200726
48294CB00003B/1180